P9-CBF-664

The Secret of Me

"On rare occasions one reads a book that is just plain touching, pulling the reader in and allowing one to feel what the character feels. Here is such a book.... This tenderly written book ... can be enjoyed by all."

—*VOYA*

"Always honest and alive ... a brave book."

—Adam Bagdasarian

"Strong feelings are conveyed in few words.... A special book filled with insight."   —Claire Rosser, *KLIATT*

"A sincere, at times poignant novel-in-verse reads like a memoir.... A first-rate offering."   —*Kirkus Reviews* (starred)

"Wonderfully written ... no one will ever again wonder why adoptees long so fiercely to know their biological parentage." —Norma Fox Mazer

The Girl in the Mirror

"There is an honesty, a darkness, a steel fragility in these beautifully crafted words. I suspect there are few readers who would not be swept up in Lizzie's destructive grief. Kearney fully engages the reader in this very fine coming-of-age novel."   —Karen Hesse

"Lizzie is wise, insightful, creative, impossible not to invest in as she spirals down and then rebounds.... A beautifully wrought story with memorable characters and true-to-life issues.   —*The Horn Book*

"Honesty to the core ... intense and personal."   —Paula Fox

Also by Meg Kearney

NOVELS ABOUT LIZZIE McLANE

The Secret of Me: A Novel in Poems (2005)

The Girl in the Mirror: A Novel in Poems and Journal Entries (2012)

POETRY

An Unkindness of Ravens (2001)

Home By Now (2009)

BOOKS FOR CHILDREN

Trouper (2013)

When You Never Said Goodbye

An Adoptee's Search for Her Birth Mother

A NOVEL IN POEMS AND JOURNAL ENTRIES

Meg Kearney

A Karen and Michael Braziller Book

PERSEA BOOKS / NEW YORK

For Elizabeth Ann Smith,
one last time
(1938–1983)

"Song of My 18th Year," "Now Two Haunt My Holidays," and "Birth Mother Villanelle" were first published in *Hunger Mountain,* the VCFA Journal of the Arts.

The author gratefully acknowledges permission to use lines from "homage to my hips" by Lucille Clifton. Copyright © 1980 by Lucille Clifton. Now appears in *The Collected Poems of Lucille Clifton 1965–2010* by Lucille Clifton, published by BOA Editions. Reprinted by permission of Curtis Brown, Ltd.

Persea Books, Inc.
277 Broadway
New York, New York 10007

Library of Congress Cataloging-in-Publication Data
Names: Kearney, Meg, author.
Title: When you never said good-bye : an adoptee's search for her birth mother : a novel in poems and journals / Meg Kearney.
Description: New York : Persea Books, [2017] | "A Karen and Michael Braziller book." | Sequel to: The girl in the mirror. | Summary: "A student at NYU in Greenwich Village, Liz McLane, pursues her dream of becoming a poet while searching for and ultimately finding her birth mother. Based on the author's experiences. Includes an autobiographical afterword."—Provided by publisher. | Includes bibliographical references.
Identifiers: LCCN 2016039183 | ISBN 978-0-89255-479-9 (hardcover : alk. paper)
Subjects: | CYAC: Novels in verse. | Adoption—Fiction. | Birthmothers—Fiction. | Universities and colleges—Fiction. | New York (N.Y)—Fiction.
Classification: LCC PZ7.5.K43 Wh 2017 | DDC [Fic]—dc23
LC record available at https://lccn.loc.gov/2016039183

Book design and composition by Rita Lascaro
Typeset in Palatino and Lucida Handwriting
Manufactured in the United States of America
First Edition

Contents

When You Never Said Goodbye

Prologue: Song of My 18th Year

Back when my heart was a little red jewel—
before my longings or long limbs were formed—
my mother, just nineteen, was fated to choose:
should she keep me, or give me away.

Now people say I'm a fact-blind fool. She did
what she did—why search for her now? I have
a blessed life. I'm still young, still in school.
She's a secret, and should stay that way.

But I'm a seeker of the past—sometimes
a breaker of rules. Maybe, just maybe
I am like her: brown curls and brown eyes
now two of the clues. *And maybe,* I say,

she's a seeker, too.

Now Two Haunt My Holidays

It's Christmas Eve. Already into the gin,
my brother Bob attempts to make us all

laugh while the turkey bakes. "What
comes before Christmas Eve?" Kate,

my chef-sister, makes gravy, rolls
her eyes. I don't. At least Bob's trying.

"Okay, what?" I ask. Mom sips tea,
focused on my father's ghost. He lingers

in this kitchen like bright, ethereal
moonlight. It takes away our appetites.

As if Mom isn't thin enough. "Christmas
Adam!" Bob says. I hear Kate groan but

I just want to cry. Dad was the king
of corny jokes. It is our first Christmas

without him. It used to be just my birth
mother who hovered over holidays,

silent and faceless. Like an outcast
no one would name. But not a ghost.

Not dead. Not like Dad. I might meet
her, someday. But Dad? Never again.

"Let's be thankful," Mom finally says,
"that we had him at all." We nod. Amen.

Journal Entry #2162: Day After Christmas

I thought my birth mother might be my Christmas present. That turned out to be like waiting for the real Santa Claus to show.

It's been 121 days since I registered. All three sites—International Soundex, the Adoptees' Liberty Movement Association, and the one in NY State—said it could take days, or it could take months before a match is made with my birth mother. That is IF, if she's registered, too. But with each passing day, I doubt more and more that she is.

How did I go from being a kid who loves Christmas to being a college student who almost dreads it? Even seeing Tim yesterday soothed but didn't cheer me. He gave me a silver bracelet and a kiss that tasted like hot chocolate, and all I could do was weep on his new blue button-down.

We all went to morning Mass—Mom, Kate, Bob, and I—and tried to sing "Silent Night" and "Come Let Us Adore Him"—Dad's favorite hymns. Back home again, carols just annoyed us. We stared at the blinking tree, hesitated to open gifts as if each one was a toy we knew was broken. That's when the idea came to me. Over dinner I said, "We don't need a tree or carols or a Yule log. What we need is a dog."

Everyone agreed. We do need furry, four-legged joy. We need wet, sloppy kisses and excuses to take long walks along our snowy road. Today we climbed in Mom's car, drove to our local shelter, and came home with a boy named Butter. So another adoptee with a mystery for a past has joined this fatherless family.

It's good timing, getting Butter. Kate took the 3:42 train back to the city, and Bob flies to CA tomorrow. Mom and I leave for NYU on Sunday, then she'll head back home to New Hook to what would have been an empty house—but won't be, thanks to the puppy. And I'll be in New York. THE place to be a poet. The last place I saw my birth mother. Okay, I was only five months old when she gave me up. But the poet Stanley Kunitz said "the blood remembers" such things. My blood remembers. That will help me find her. It must.

Lucky

Dog breath—that's what I wake to—Butter
thumping his paws on the edge of my bed,
licking me to death.   *Where am I?*
Right. I'm home.   *And the time?*
After nine! Tim is coming at ten so we can
spend the day. (He goes away again
tomorrow—some golf thing.) Swinging
my legs out of bed, I thank Butter with a kiss
on his head, then run for the shower.

Florida sun has deepened Tim's half-
Mexican skin to the dark copper of an old
penny. *Plenty of girls must be after you,*
I think as Butter and I greet him at the door.
Tim's hug feels better than I'd hoped for;
his kiss, more welcome than a woodstove
in winter. He offers a hand to Butter, who
sits down to shake it. "Let me know if you
want me to take this dog to Miami," Tim

teases Mom, who's come from the kitchen
to say hello. She's wearing the new scarf
I gave her for Christmas, all greens and blues
to accent her auburn hair. "Apparently
he's already earned his degree," Mom says,
then asks about Tim's father and brother
George. Tim tells her about George's new
wheelchair, a special kind that rolls on sand
so they can bring him to the beach. I sneak

a stare at Tim while he speaks—his jeans,
his cream fisherman's net sweater that shows
off his tan. Is this man really with me?
We head out to snowshoe at the State Park,
and I catch a glimpse of my face in the mirror
by the door. My new black sweater doesn't

help—I'm white as paper. Church-white
with monk-brown curls. *You,* I silently tell
my reflection, *are one lucky girl.*

Haiku for Tim: Snowshoeing, Catskill Mountain State Park

Pine scent, cardinal
on a birch branch. Remember?
Your lips, blue as snow.

Off to College, Take 2

Once again my Subaru's jammed with stuff
I'm bringing to college, only this time we had
to leave enough room for Butter on the back-
seat. Once again my friend Jan is here to see
me off, laughing as Mom bugs me about
the back window being blocked by pillows
and bags, only this time our friend Jade is
here, too, wishing me luck at NYU. Once
again I climb into the driver's seat, Mom
beside me with her tea. Once again friends
wave as I beep and drive away, then lightly
touch my charm necklace to make sure it's
still there—only this time neither Mom nor
I say we wish Dad were here, too. He is.
And so am I, pants Butter, planting kisses
in my ear.

The Other Me (Or, Why I'm Going to New York Instead of Back to Syracuse University)

The Other Me was at SU three weeks when she realized
my mistake. Instead of following my head as she always
does, she should've followed my heart's ache, as the *other*
Other Me would make me do. At SU I thought I'd become
a reporter—make a living by being a writer for a newspaper
or TV. It took Journalism 101 to discover (make that, whack
me over the head with) Rule Number One: "stick to the facts."
In poems, you can make things up as long as what you say
is true. I'm an aspiring poet—what could I do? Transfer
to NYU. What better place to grow in my art than
Manhattan? And what better place to learn where I came
from than the city where I was born? So here I am, following
my heart. (And yes, birth mother, following *you*.)

Doesn't It Figure

Doesn't it figure—
we're already on
the West Side
Highway—Mom's
driving now—we're
in Manhattan, nearly
there when somehow
she decides to say,
"I suppose you haven't
heard from any
registries? It's been
a while since I've
asked." *Three weeks,*
I think, but just say
"No," gaze at the bleak
morning haze. "Didn't
think so," Mom says,
but she doesn't let it
go. "I wonder—after
the fall you've had—"
(*All I need is a lecture,*
I think, watching
the streets plus her
from the corner of one
eye.) "Maybe you
should just focus
on your studies? Forget
about registries for
a while?" She tries
to smile. "Forty-second
Street," I say, as in
someone's watching
where we're going.
I try to keep calm.
"Right—we'll go left
on Fourteenth," she

responds with a mock
kind of brightness, like
a nightlight in a dungeon.
"So, what do you think?"
That you need to see
a shrink? I want to say...
Don't go there. I swear
I try to stop myself, even
wave one hand as if to
clear the air, but still I
blurt, "You don't get it.
You say you do, but you
don't. Kate didn't at first.
Only Dad. *He* would have
totally supported me, this
search!" Mom's face
looks wooden and red
as if I'd slapped it.
Which I kind of did,
mentioning Dad like that.
But what did she expect?
Now we're both wrecks.
A kind of sadness fills
my veins like poison sap.
Butter whimper-groans
from the back seat. "Good
Butter," Mom soothes, but
won't look at me. We turn
left on Fourteenth Street,
right on Hudson, Bleecker—
I should be psyched, about
to meet my roommate Rhett,
about to start my dream.
Instead my cheeks are wet;
my heart feels like a sun about
to set. "Left," I instruct, my
voice tinged with regret. "I'm
sorry, Lizzie—this isn't how
I want to leave you, and I only

meant—" "I know," I say,
determined not to pout, spirits
slightly rising as we turn
right on Washington Square
South, then left and here we
are with a zillion other cars
at Goddard Hall. Mom stops
the car; Butter's panting—he
sees trees. Mom turns to look
at me. "I *do* understand,
Lizzie, and I love you. Only—
I worry." Her voice is shaky.
As we hug I whisper that
I love her, too, and now Butter
tries to join us, head popping
between our seats. Mom
slips him a treat as we laugh,
relieved we haven't totally
destroyed this day. Now
I can't believe we're *here*.
"End of the road for me,"
I tell Butter, scratching his ears.

Hello, New York; Hello, Rhett Gilbert Driskell

I.

Parking lot. Tail-gate party. Traffic-
jam. Flea market. Washington Square
East could be any of these. Cars line up
on both sides of the street, purple
and white balloons flounce in the breeze
above matching fabric signs that read
"GODDARD HALL:
NYU WELCOMES YOU."

Dressed in jeans, heels, and NYU
sweatshirts (even though it's freezing),
three girls go by rolling huge plastic
buckets filled with duffel bags and boxes;
two more carry big shopping bags
decorated with reindeer and elves.
Beyond them, a boy in a Stoned Crows
T-shirt pulls a suitcase while nearby

a man hugs a girl goodbye. I stare
amazed as a guy with purple spiked
hair glides by playing something
classical on a violin. While Mom takes
Butter to the park for a "break" (Butter
sniffing every bit of ground, every
mound of dirty snow), I try to shake
off our little tiff—how weird things
get when we talk about my search—
and again take in the fact that I'm here.

II.

"You should have seen it last fall,"
a voice with a tiny drawl says. "You
never would've scored a spot this fast."

Twirling around, I see a girl with stylish
red glasses, dark hair as straight and short
as mine is curly and long. "Rhett?"
I'm sure she is but—I try to decide
whether she's five feet one or two.
(My Tall Girl Syndrome means I always
try to take a mental measure.) "You
didn't guess I'm so vertically challenged,"
she says, smiling. An Indian man walks by,
a suitcase in each hand. "You look just like
your picture, Liz." She offers her hand to
shake, but we hug instead. She smells
expensive, like Chanel. "I know your
voice from all our calls," I say, "and saw
your picture on Facebook—" I hesitate,
unsure. "It's the glasses," Rhett explains,
touching one finger to the scarlet frame.
"I was too tired to put in my eyes." That's
what Kate calls her contacts, so I'm not
confused. Walking full around my car
she asks no one in particular, "Where
to begin?" "It doesn't matter," I answer,
glancing toward the park, "but first you
need to meet Mom. And Butter."

It's like being one of a few bees left in a hive, knowing more than half my fellow bees are somewhere warm, doing their flower thing. But they'll be back for spring ... the rest of us are here for January Term.

About 200 Freshmen (and women!) live here, mostly English/Liberal Studies majors.

Rhett claims: "Nice people, tight community!" "City excursions!" "Theater, museums, poetry readings!" Most people hang out in the hallways of each floor @ night ... which floor depends on your mood/interests.

7th Floor (where we live):
Quiet, most private. Window in hall: can see Washington Square Park, kind of. Walls are a happy-face yellow. Smell of burned popcorn.

6th Floor:
Intellectuals congregate here, talk politics (political science minors), world history, food/cooking, comic books & graphic novels. Avoid talk of sports, especially if you're from New England (Red Sox, Patriots + Yankees, Giants = fights worse than ones about religion). Odor of antiseptic? Poster of Michelle Obama on somebody's door.

5th Floor:
Only quiet because it's noon on Saturday & January Term. Come here for arts & crafts (origami—at least 1,000 paper swans taped to a bulletin board). Pictionary, concerts (violins, guitars, African drums, mandolins).

Smell of oranges, antiseptic. Floors just cleaned? Someone burning (unauthorized) candles?

4th Floor: "Still discovering its *raison d'être*.*" —Rhett
* Looked this up: means "reason for existence."
Fashion shows (something Japanese?), séances, hip-hop/rap, chess, cheese

doodles, face painting, thumb wrestling. Rumor: ballroom dancing this spring.

That antiseptic smell covering up sweat. Note on someone's door: "BEWARE OF ZOMBIES ALL YE WHO ENTER HERE."

3rd Floor:
"Party Central," by vote last October, post-11 p.m. nightly except Mondays. Alcohol not allowed but "we make do." Lots of music here, too. "And cute guys."

Two doors show off Mind of Snow posters, one signed by the band. A mop leans against the wall. I think I smell pot, but the smell of coffee overpowers everything else.

2nd Floor:
"Study hall." "Study buddies." Serious students—usually lots here. If you need quiet/solo focus, go to library or 7th floor. Guy named Calvin hangs here a lot but lives on 3 and I should meet him (!?). Lots of doors have posters: Einstein; bottom half of a head with daisies growing out of the top; Charlie Chaplin; some guy with a cello; B.G. Parker, lead singer of Boston Cure.

That Clorox smell again, plus something sweet—cookies? Chocolate.

Ground Floor:
Wi-Fi. Starbucks: "one of the busiest in Manhattan." "Don't think you can grab coffee running to class—line is usually out the door, sometimes stretches around the corner." If desperate, "Sam and Calvin make great coffee" (3rd floor).

Definitely smell coffee; something spicy. And heat.

Basement:
Laundry room. Some machines always broken. Good luck getting washer/dryer unless come at weird time. Two guys sit on washing machines, staring at their phones.

Lounge! Empty. TV works. "Lending library": take a book, leave a book.

Parties often start here, but by 2 a.m. wind up on 3rd floor.

Clorox again, but also a musty smell. And flowers? Detergent.

After our tour, we head to St. Mark's Place: Thai food at Klong, big lunch for $7.50! That's when Rhett explains why I lucked out and got a room in Goddard—the girl who was supposed to be her roommate in the fall (Sarah somebody) went AWOL. Seems Sarah called the day before classes started to say she was on her way to NY, but never made it past NJ. Something about a boyfriend at Rutger's.

Goddard Hall *rocks*. Right on the PARK. Already wish I could spend all four years here.

Perfect Roommates

Rhett says *I'm* the reason her first roommate
didn't show. I'm leaning on the half wall
that separates our desks, noting it's tall
enough to give us each privacy—great
in a room so small—and if I'm up late
studying, my light won't bother her at all.

I just feel lucky that some girl last fall
went running after a boy. Rhett says it's fate,
because not only do we have a lot
in common, we're also both neat (couldn't live
with a slob), don't snore, don't hog the bathroom,
and even though we like to party, we put
grades and school first. She wipes down our fridge,
full of Diet Coke, while I grab the broom.

Three texts from Tim today (so far):
1) MISS U
2) warm here but would rather be on snowshoes w/ u
3) saw someone writing w/ one of those black pencils & thought of you

Note to self: stock up on Mirado Black Warrior #2s! Village Stationery will have them if NYU's bookstore doesn't.

Text from Bob: "Hope u & Mom made it to NY w/o bloodshed. Like new job but CA = surreal. Like the moon. Good luck & call/text whenever. Mom sends daily photos of Butter."

So he gets those photos, too—Butter sleeping by the fire, Butter shaking his frog toy. Butter holding his bone between his paws like a kid holding an ice-cream cone. Butter's bone, which he leaves standing on end in the middle of the living room floor like a little tower.

Bob feels farther than the moon. He won't ask about the search. Kate says he worries I'm setting myself up to get burned. Last fall, when Kate told him I'd registered with ALMA and the adoption registery run by NY State's Department of Health, he asked her, "Why would Lizzie's birth mother ask for a closed adoption, then years later register her name so she could be found?" I wish Kate hadn't shared that. Maybe it was *her* way of warning me not to get my hopes up—while blaming it on Bob.

Like Bob, Rhett never stands at the sink when she brushes her teeth. Bob watches TV. Rhett waltzes out of the bathroom, checks her phone, twirls around a couple of times, then heads back into the bathroom to spit.

Isn't it funny—I have no idea what Tim does when he brushes his teeth. Rhett already asked me if I'm a virgin. She's not. She asked if Tim is, too—and that stopped me. I'm sure he's not, though I've never asked. He's had other girlfriends . . . I just dated Peter. Rhett said, "Probably best not to think about it."

Yup.

Postcard from Cathy in Mexico

Lizzie! Can I still call you that? I know
at college you switched to Liz. Was
happy to hear you're at NYU at last—
where you were meant to be all along.
By summer I'll leave Aguas Calientes
& join you in NYC! Columbia said yes,
so I'm on my way ... my parents can't
wait for me to be home, though they're
proud of the work I've done here
at the orphanage & how I've become
determined to be a Dr. (They think
I'll change my mind about working
with the poor.) Write if you can—esp.
if you hear from the registries!

Con amor,
Cathy

ps love WA Sq Park, too—we'll hang
there in June!

Ode to Washington Square Park

(After doing some online research)

First owned by Indians, then freed
slaves—former burial ground, parade
ground, Potter's Field—Washington
Square, living here, makes me feel
rich. Who else could live in Greenwich
Village where Fifth Avenue ends
under a seventy-seven-foot marble
arch, where sand artists and jugglers
meet puppeteers and break dancers,
where Mark Twain chatted with Robert
Louis Stevenson, where London
plane trees shade dog runs and play-
grounds, where a huge fountain
invites waders and toe-dippers and
spectators of every nation—students,
lovers, loners, families on vacation—
no matter what the season? Note
to self: no reason to live anywhere else!

Journal Entry #2165

Goddard Hall: 79 Washington Sq. East

My neighborhood map.

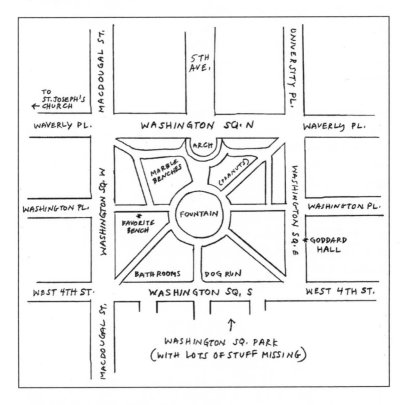

Inscription on arch: "Let us raise a standard to which the wise and the honest can repair. The event is in the hand of God.—Washington"

(The "event!" My search? Maybe I should be going to church more often ... that always seems to center me.)

Birth Mother Villanelle

She must be here in New York, my first home—
this isn't some adoptee fantasy.
I feel it in my gut, my bones.

The only other mother I have ever known
says she, too, thinks it a possibility:
she could be here in New York, my first home—

city of concrete, of glass, of lights and stone;
island surrounded by rivers and sea.
I feel it in my gut, my bones.

This birth mother's inspired many a poem
even though she's a stranger, a mystery.
She must be here in New York, my first home

and maybe hers, too. Perhaps she never roamed,
so didn't want me growing up in *her* city.
I feel it in my gut, in my bones

that she'll welcome me, now that I'm grown.
I could be as close as the sand is to sea.
She *must* be here, in New York, our first home—
I feel it in my gut, in my bones.

Tim & I Play the Long-Distance Game

Rhett's the *best*, I tell Tim. She nearly brought
as many electric candles as I did. She's an animal
lover, too. He laughs when I tell him how Butter
charmed her with his paw-shake trick. "Charmed
you, too," I say. His voice goes soft. "You should
have come to Miami." "And what would I do,"
I gently tease, "go to the beach instead of
the Bowery?" "You love the Poetry Club more
than me," he counters, breathing as he speaks
in a way I know well. "You're swinging an imaginary
golf club right now," I say. "True ..." He exhales.
"But I'd rather have my arms around you."

No More Shame

Jan sends a text: *No news yet?*
No news STILL, I text back,
Must not be registered.
With that, my phone rings.
Jan. She's always had

a knack for knowing when
I need her voice. "She might
not think it's her choice
this time," Jan says. I ask
what she means. "Last week

at group, Joe claimed some
birth mothers are so ashamed
they gave their babies up,
they think they have no right
to search." Cripes. I want

my other mother to feel lots
of things, but not that she
doesn't deserve to find me.
Not shame. I played that
game long enough for both

of us. "It's from all that guilt
crap they feed you in church,"
Jan says. I don't think so,
but don't say that—Jan's
in a rush now; she has to go.

Regret

Dad went to NYU, walked
these streets, sat in this park,
too—studied, partied, sweet-
talked girls, and who knows
what else. I beat myself up
now, stew because he can't
take the train and meet me
here; can't say, *My view was
this. There, I'd meet my
friends. Once I knew the best
places to eat* ... I don't have
a clue because I didn't ask,
or treat his past like something
to treasure, to write down, keep
to soothe me when I'm blue.

Journal Entry #2166

Rhett says it's good I've come for January session, before everyone's back—I can get to know a few people in Goddard and my classes before the pace picks up.

Only taking two classes—both seem fascinating already:

1) "It's Okay to Laugh: Contemporary Poetry with a Sense of Humor" taught by professor Steven Rochester. Everyone calls him "Professor R." He reminds me of Uncle Rob—brown hair pulled into a pony tail, a closely cropped beard, built like a runner/biker. And he does make us all laugh. Reading poems by Billy Collins, Theodore Roethke, Heather McHugh, James Tate, Ron Padgett, Tess Gallagher. He also challenges us to find poems that fit the topic. I've been reading some of Professor R's poems at the library, and some are very funny, and all are very good.

2) "The Necessary Munro." Randall James is the most brilliant man I've ever met and, I realize, my first African-American teacher. (Geez, how sad is *that?*) He's very handsome but has a very large head, which makes sense as he needs a place to store all those brains. We're reading Alice Munro's short stories to "explore craft" and "themes" (death, feminism, survival . . .).

I'd better hunker down and work—lock that party girl inside me in a closet. It's not good enough that I promised Mom that I would. I have to promise *myself*. If I start drinking like I did at those parties last summer, I'm done for. As it is, something tells me that this winter/spring will be crazier than a ride down a mountain in a car with no brakes.

Jan Sends Me to a Facebook Page

where a girl our age has posted a photo
of herself holding a sign that reads (Oh
no, my heart bleeds for her): "Looking

for my birth mother," then proceeds to
list when and where she was born,
and pleads for people to share her post.
Most of the comments say, "Good luck!"

and "Glad to spread the word!" *What
guts she has to ask all the world for help,*
I think. I share her story, but ignore Jan's
question, "Give this a try?" Not my style.

I wish that girl a bunch of luck—I really
do—but don't have the pluck to post
about my search. I'd rather be a lion's
lunch at the Central Park Zoo.

One Could Do Worse

"If you like Faulkner and Flannery O'Connor,
you'll adore Alice Munro," says Rhett, who is
now the most well-read person I know. We're in
the park, people-watching and comparing notes
on our professors. I quote Professor James
in my best Southern drawl: "Ms. Munro has
revolutionized the architecture of the short story..."
"Lucky you!" beams Rhett, meaning it. I shift
on the towel she brought to sit on so our butts
won't freeze on the marble bench, one reason
why I prefer the wooden ones under the trees.
"Please," I whine, feeling behind Rhett and half
my classmates. "I've only read Faulkner's
'The Bear' in school, and am clueless about
O'Connor." *Where will I find the time to catch
up?* "Well, don't drop out yet," says Rhett,
reading my mind. She's done that twice today,
first just by suggesting we come here. "Let's
go," I say, "My butt is ice, and that woman's
too weird." Rhett follows my stare—a granny
in a long purple coat is feeding squirrels
from her handbag. "They are in her purse!"
I whisper. "That's Squirrel Lady," says Rhett,
standing with a grin. "One could do worse
than having *squirrels* steal from your purse."

Journal Entry #2167: January 10

Called Jan to wish her a happy birthday. She liked the anthology I gave her—couldn't believe there are so many poems about cars. She asked if next time I'm home, I'll read her some—she said hearing them out loud somehow makes them easier to understand.

That made me think back to slumber party days, making my friends listen to poems while we lounged around in pajamas. Our sleeping bags in a circle like bright flower petals, our heads pointing toward the center where we kept our phones and bowl of popcorn. I always felt over the moon when they wanted to hear more Lucille Clifton or Anne Sexton.

I did suggest that Jade could read poems to her while she works, but Jan said she's not a very good listener when she's in the middle of a brake job. Jade probably hangs out at Mack's Garage like I used to do. Sits in the shop on my old stool—probably studies that same poster hanging on the wall, "How to Change a Tire," while Jan's head hides under the hood of someone's Ford Focus.

What's that ache I feel? Nostalgia? Jealousy? *Both.*

Before we hung up, Jan wished me a happy "Adoption Day." I didn't know what to say. She's one of the few people who know that January 10 is the day my parents brought me home from The New York Foundling. Ever since I learned that last summer, when—at the start of my search—The Foundling sent my non-identifying information, I've felt different somehow. As if I were suddenly trying to stand on a log as it rushed down a river. That mind-blowing letter making the river churn with its facts. Like, Your birth mother was a brown-haired, brown-eyed college student with Scottish blood who had a hard time giving you up, but we can't tell you her name or where she lives. And oh yeah, your birth father's ancestors were French, and he has no idea you even exist.

All these spinning details—when what I really wanted (or *thought* I wanted) was her name and address. I guess those would be defined as "identifying." Against the rules. But I like knowing I'm Scottish and

French. French on my *b.f.'s* side ... he was probably a charmer. Romantic. Aren't French men known for that?

I told Jan that I'd love to read her some poems from the anthology next time I'm home. She realizes my family never celebrated—never *mentioned* Adoption Days for Kate or Bob or me. It seems weird to start now. As weird as it would be if I suddenly started posting about all this adoption stuff on Facebook. It's taken me this long to be open about it with my best friends—it might take decades for me to share it with the world!

Does Mom know what day this is? ... I won't ask. It's enough that Jan knows; she remembered.

Ms. Guitar in Washington Square Park

The sound stopped me—a woman playing guitar
and singing a song I'd soon come to know.
She was a stranger, yet her voice was so familiar.

Lots of us were in the park, even though it was winter—
it wasn't cold. Sun had melted most of the snow.
The sound stopped me—a woman playing guitar

and her voice—dusky, but strong and clear.
I was supposed to meet Rhett, but didn't want to go.
She was a stranger, yet her voice was familiar—

I could have sworn I'd heard it before.
Maybe one time with Kate? I didn't think so,
but the sound stopped me. A woman playing guitar

isn't odd. "Had that dream again of asters . . ."
she sang. I closed my eyes. "The wind blows . . ."
She was a stranger! Yet her voice was familiar—

it seemed impossible I hadn't ever met her.
I'd be late. Rhett would understand, though:
The sound stopped me, I'd say. *A woman playing guitar—*
she was a stranger, yet her voice was so familiar . . .

Rhett & I Wind Up at The Rock

As planned, Rhett's waiting for me on the sidewalk
outside Goddard Hall. She's changed out of her
sweatshirt and is wearing boots, jeans, a black
turtleneck, and a beat-up brown leather
jacket, a gift from her ex-boyfriend Chris.
She glances up from her phone. "You're late."
"I know," I say, "I'm sorry! There was this
woman in the park—I'm never late—
but her voice—she was playing a guitar—"

Rhett looks up. "Yeah, her name—Liz, are you
okay?" I just stare at her. "There's a bar
near Astor Place where they won't card you
if it's before four," she says, grabbing my
arm. A bar? Who's going to argue? Not I.

My First Time at The Rock, Where I Tell Rhett About the Woman in the Park and She Tells Me Her Life Story

I. Recognition

Gray cement steps and a black iron rail
lead down one flight to the dark door
of The Rock. Inside it's dimly lit

and smells of wood, wool, and the steak
fries they cook in a tiny kitchen behind
the bar—slices of potato fried golden

brown, slices thick as a lumberjack's
fingers. That's what I say, "Thick as
a lumberjack's fingers," when the waitress

sets the basket on the table between Rhett
and me. "What do you know about
lumberjacks?" says Rhett, and I say,

"Nothing except for Paul Bunyan and his
blue ox." My Dad used to tell stories,
I explain, and out spills the tale of his heart

attack last spring and my drinking binges
last summer and thinking maybe I wouldn't
go to college and my missing him above

everything. The waitress comes back
with the two vodka gimlets Rhett ordered,
no questions asked. I cross my legs, sit up

straighter. Then Rhett tells me her story
and it's as if a door's opening between us—
we're each walking, talking through it,

one toward the other, discovering we're not
strangers at all but instead silently exclaiming,
Oh, you! I've been looking all over for you.

II. Rhett's Story (In Her Voice, with Her Permission)

It was always summertime
until I was nine. My brother
Don and I rode bikes in sunshine,
climbed trees, raced with our mother

on roller skates through the town
park. When our father was home,
our mother played piano; we sang "Down
the Old Ohio" and "Where the Buffalo Roam."

Then Mom got sick, and it was fall.
We learned the word "chemo." Her skin
turned weird colors. Then it was all
about hospitals, doctors, radiation.

But the last leaf fell. She was gone.
Winter set in fast—there was no more
piano, no roller skating, no sun.
Our world had been drained of color.

Dad took his truck on longer hauls
than ever, leaving us with Uncle Zack.
Zack drank lots of beer, played softball,
taught us how to play gin and black jack.

By the time we were fifteen, sixteen,
Don and I were failing in school.
We were drinking, smoking, played a mean
game of rummy. It's all a bad dream

now, 'cause spring arrived that year.
Dad met Janet, brought her home

to meet us. Day one, it was clear
she liked us. She couldn't be Mom,

but we liked her, too. So Dad
quit his truck, got a job in town.
He bought all the roses the florist had;
Janet and I chose her wedding gown.

Now they're married. We call Janet "Moms."
In the Navy, Don says things happen for a reason.
Sometimes I long for those summer days—songs,
bikes, skates—but everything has its season.

III. Mystery

It's quarter to four and we're on our second
gimlet. My head's swirly; I'm feeling giddy
by the time I remember to ask about that
musician in the park. Rhett whips out
a pack of matches from her purse, lights
the candle on our table, a booth near
the dart board along the bar's back wall.
She is a soul sister, I think, and she says
she rates bars and restaurants on their level
of darkness. I hold up my drink and we
clink glasses. "So that singer—in the park—"
I say. "Her name starts with an R," Rhett
says. I ask how she knows her. Turns out
she doesn't really, but "Sam's brother
Dan who's a senior says she used to play
in clubs around the city." "Well, Ms. R
sang this *totally* amazing song. And her
voice blew me away—it sounded so,
so familiar," I say. Rhett wants to know
if that's why I had that look on my face
when we met earlier today. The vodka's
made me spacey but now my reaction
to Ms. R's voice seems over the top.
"Did I?" I say. Rhett looks at me funny

but then checks her phone. Time's up—
they'll be carding us soon. We slip out,
head back to our room. Outside is so
bright! We'd forgotten it was still
afternoon. At The Rock, every day
is always a kind of blurry night.

Tim

Tim is a golf course in spring—wide open,
welcoming views edged by pines chiming
with bird song. He is the song, too—a flutey
melody backed by guitar strum sure to soothe
the bluest part of you. True alchemist, he takes
that blue, makes it shine like moonlight on
the darkest night until you rise, a new sun
inside you. Rain, not even snow can chill you
then—though there he is, making a shelter
of his arms just to be sure. So you move in
closer. Wonder about the future. And suddenly
you know as sure as you can sing your own
heart's hymn: you'll be seen, you'll be loved,
you'll be safe with him. All that waits beyond
this world you've made—well, let it come.

Journal Entry #2168

News from Jan: Joe just left on some big trip to Brazil, so the Adoption Support Group won't meet again until next month. She sounded surprisingly disappointed. Here Jade and I practically had to drag her to that first meeting, and now she's bummed she can't go. Maybe she's disappointed because Jade is?

BUT: at the last meeting, a woman talked about how she found her birth mother. One of the first things she did was look up her birth record at the New York Public Library. She said they keep records of everyone born in Manhattan!

Got to get to the NYPL soon. Asked Jan if she and Jade would come down and go with me. "We're there," Jan said. I want them to meet Rhett, too, but Jan didn't say anything when I mentioned that—just asked about trains, about where we should meet. Looks like Saturday works for all three of us.

In some ways, Jade's friendship is like this city—some neighborhoods I know as well as I know my own home town, and yet there are others I'm just starting to explore. What I like best about her is how she seems to know ways to make Jan smile when no one else can. That Jan—*she* can be one rough neighborhood. But if I drew a map of it, in its center would be one HUGE heart.

If Rhett wonders why I don't invite *her* on my "mission" to the library— well, I need to explain before I go about my being adopted, how I have that in common with Jan and Jade. I need to explain about my search. Why is it always—still—so hard to talk about this stuff with people who don't know, people outside my family and closest friends? Maybe I should just give Rhett copies of the two manuscripts of poems I've written, *The Secret of Me* and *The Girl in the Mirror*. Those will explain everything. And speaking of secrets, I already sense that Rhett can keep one. She'll understand that I need to be the one to tell my story to people, *my way*, if I tell it at all.

The Hamster in My Family

Adoption's no longer the proverbial elephant
in the room, which everyone pretends isn't
there. We've come that far. Still, my search
is like a hamster in a cage no one cares for
but me. Brown and beige and kind of sad,
it runs endlessly on its little wheel. Once
in a while, Mom or Bob pad by and whisper,
"Good hamster!" Kate, at least, stops to ask,
"How's hamster feel today?" Maybe it's my
fate, but I'm the only one who feeds it, makes
sure it has water, reaches in through the steel
bars to pet its head. Everyone seems content
with this but me. They want hamster to stay
where it is, not let it out. They want our lives
to remain the same. What will they do when
I open that cage, when I give that hamster—
when I can give my first mother—a name?

In the Laundry Room:
I Meet Rhett's Nemesis

Rhett thought noon on Sunday
was the perfect time to catch
the laundry room empty, but
turns out she was wrong. All
the washers are taken except
two, not counting one that's
broken. "What else is new?"
says Rhett about the Out
of Order sign. We're sorting
which clothes really need
cleaning while I tell her more
about Tim—how we haven't
gone out super long, but I'm
crazy about him, how he golfs
and plays guitar, how he likes
poetry and goes to school so far
away at UM, how we agreed
we're free to date other people,
but neither of us wants to. Rhett
looks relieved as I blabber on,
and then stops, touches my arm.
"I bet that's why you like Ms. R's
playing so much—it makes you
think of Tim." Why didn't I think
of that before? "I'll tell him—"
I start to say, but Rhett's smile
has turned into a thin, straight line.
Behind us is a girl I didn't see
come in—she's short like Rhett,
but has long red hair instead of
short brown. Tension rises
like hair on a dog's back. We
watch as she opens every dryer
then spins around. "Oh, hi,"
she pants as if she's out of breath.

"Rhett, Sam told me you got
a roommate—someone from north
of here, a *country* girl," she says,
slowly twirling to face me. Since
when did the word "country" sound
like "manure"? Or, more like it,
"shit"? "Liz," I say, offering my hand.
There's a trace of surprise in her eyes
as we shake. I give her hand a firm
squeeze—just like my dad taught me.
In case she forgets my name, she'll
remember this. Turns out her name's
Louise. She empties all the just-finished
washers; proceeds to hog all the dryers.

In the Lounge, Waiting for Dryers

"What's with her?" I whisper as Rhett flicks off
the TV that no one's watching.
"Where does that witch get off?

She doesn't even know me!" I'm so mad
I could spit. "Welcome to my world,"
says Rhett, "But I'm just glad

you're on my team. I needed an ally
with a mean, country-girl handshake."
That makes us laugh, but I'm

still wondering why a perfect stranger
(who thinks she owns the laundry room)
would be so rude. "For her

to assume she knows anything about
me, that I'm some country cow-tipper—"
"Calm down," Rhett says. "No doubt

she hasn't a clue who she's dealing with."
Rhett's looking through the books people
can take or leave. "Edith

Wharton!" Rhett holds up the book like a trophy
over her head. "Don't you just love her?
She's not my century—

my focus is nineteenth—but you must read
her since you love New York."
I say I will, but I need

to read some stories by Alice Munro
and poems by Billy Collins
first. We see Louise go

by, carrying an empty basket. Her
extensive wardrobe must be dry
by now, but to be sure

we follow her, watch her open then slam
each dryer, then she's gone at last.
"So Rhett," I ask. "Who's Sam?"

Journal Entry #2169

Scene: Back in our room

Still PEEVED after the laundry room incident with Louise, I'm leaning on Rhett's desk. She's on her bed.

Me: I should have told her I was born right *here* in Greenwich Village. Just a few blocks away!

Rhett: Louise? Forget her. She has no manners unless there's a cute guy nearby. Oh, wait—she has no manners then, either. She just hides it better. Guys are clueless.

Me: I should have said I've been coming to the city all my life. My sister lives here! She and Bob and I were all born at St. Vincent's Hospital!

Rhett: Really? Cool! Too bad they tore it down. But they left its shell—you can kind of tell what it looked like.

Me: That's so sad I can't even walk by it right now. But I bet I know Manhattan as well as she does, even if she did grow up here. I should have said—

Rhett (taking a photo of me with her phone): "Liz McLane, 'bursting with the belated eloquence of the inarticulate.'"

Me: Huh?

Rhett: Edith Wharton. *Age of Innocence.*

[Note: when I asked about this Sam person, Rhett said, "Just a friend." He seems to come up in an awful lot of conversations. Almost as often as his roommate, Calvin.]

Pigeons in Winter

Brown, white, filthy birds
in the park: where does snow end
and pigeon begin?

Journal Entry #2170

After reading it at the library, I just had to buy Professor R's book *Redemption Arcade*. My favorite poems are "Sugar on Toast" and "Making Love with You for the First Time"—which is so freakin' funny I had to read it to Tim.

The first three stanzas:

> It's like returning home after being away
> a long time: first, all that anticipation—
>
> and once there, everything both familiar
> and new. We make do on my old twin bed—
>
> I cry YES! You cry MORE! Then
> my mother knocks loudly on the door.

At that point, Tim let out a belly laugh and didn't stop laughing until the poem was over.

The poem's in couplets. Maybe to insinuate how usually it "takes two to tango"? Maybe. Using just everyday language, Prof. R is able to take any subject and make it hysterically funny. And human. He makes it possible for us to laugh at ourselves. His poem "Sperm Count" made us both laugh—I could barely get through it.

Tim asked to hear the "Making Love" poem again. Then he said—I could tell he had this sly smile on his face—"Guess we'll have to avoid your mom's house the first time, too."

... I opened my mouth, but no words came out. I was glad then that we *weren't* using FaceTime. My cheeks could have glowed in the dark.

"Guess so . . . I have to go," I stammered. Real smooth.

But now I'm thinking, *Maybe this summer . . . ?*

———

I sent Cathy a copy of "Sperm Count." Cathy always refers to her birth father as "the sperm." Like, that's all he was good for. I wonder. My non-identifying information letter from The Foundling said my b.m. had already broken up with my b.f. before she realized she was pregnant, and so she decided not to tell him. He probably doesn't know about me. If I find her, WHEN I find her, maybe I'll learn more. Maybe she even changed her mind, and is back with him now. That happened to that "Mad Girl" in group—when she found her birth parents were married, I think she wanted to hug and then kill them. But she did find two for the price of one!

Anyway, it was my b.m. I spent the first part of my life with—those nine months, those visits during the five months I was in foster care. She and I have the connection, not him. Whoever, wherever he is. My blood remembers *her.*

Ms. R in the Park

The first time I get a good look
at her, first time I sit
across from her

on a wood bench just opposite
so I can get a good view
without being

obvious, she's playing "You've Got
a Friend." A black wool hat covers
her ears and hair.

Not one strand, not a curl peeks from
that hat. When she gazes
up at the trees

as I often do, I'm startled
by her eyes, large and dark
as my dad's were.

Larger, even, so I can't help
but stare. Her face and lips
are pale, thin, yet

I do imagine artists would
be drawn to paint that face,
those eyes, which now

stare back at me. Still singing—
"winter, spring, summer or
fall ... "—she smiles.

Clapping with my mittens on seems
weird, but I know and love
this oldies song.

Native New Yorker

(With thanks to Mom for sending me a Starbucks gift card)

I have time for one last cup
of coffee before class, so
I'm in line behind some guy
with sandy hair, summer blue
eyes, and a sketchbook under

one arm. He seems to know each
student who walks by. Despite
the graphite pencil sticking
from his back pocket, he's not
my type. Too blond. Too . . . not Tim.

"Hey, Louise!" this guy calls out.
Great, I roll my eyes. Louise
is by his side in seconds
flat. "Hey, *hel-lo,*" she says, breathy
and flushed, pretending I'm not

there. Whatever. I don't care
unless she thinks she's using
him to cut in front of me.
"Hey," he says, "you're the native
New Yorker. How do you get

up to Hudson View Gardens? West
One Hundred Eighty-third Street
and Pinehurst Avenue? Dan's
professor is reading up
there—we haven't got a clue

how to find it." Louise turns
scarlet. "It's not really my
neighborhood, but let me think,"
she stammers. "Maybe the One?"
"The A train's better," I blurt

without thinking. They both turn
to me—her eyes are shooting
darts, but she'll miss her target
this time. I just look at him.
"Try to be in the front car

if you can," I say. "When you
reach One Hundred Eighty-first
Street, walk north on the platform
to the last staircase ... " I give
detailed directions, watching

Louise seethe from the corner
of my eye as he types them
into his phone. When I'm done,
I give her my brightest smile.
She looks like she just swallowed

something vile. Am I gloating
when her phone rings and she runs
away? Yes. Yes, I am. Then
the guy says, "Thanks! Are you new?
I've never seen you—I'm Sam."

About to Tell Rhett About My Search

Where to start? With a goodbye
my body remembers but my mind
can't see? With a letter, a baby,
that murmur in my heart? A foster
mother, a foundling—no, three.
A surrender. Longing. Loyalty—
our family tree. A birthday.
A registry. *The Secret of Me.*

Journal Entry #2171

<u>Scene:</u> **2nd floor hallway**

I'm sitting with Rhett and a girl named Henri, helping them cut snowflakes out of sheets of white paper, daisy-like flowers out of yellow. The daisies remind me of Jan's hair (though for all I know, today she's dyed it orange).

When I met Henri last week, she described herself as "Half Chinese, half Czech, and half Fig Newton" (though an empty bag of Oreos lies at her feet, which don a pair of red slippers made to look like dragons—heads popping up from her toes, tails dragging behind her heels). Casually, I tell them how I finally met Sam, trying not to gloat over the scene with Louise. I expect Rhett to ask why it took me two days to tell her this (especially since we had such a personal talk last night), but she doesn't.

Rhett: That's my country girl—went straight for her jugular!

Henri: I didn't even know there *is* an A train.

Me: Kate—my sister—and I have been to Hudson View Gardens a few times for readings—

Rhett (not looking up from her snowflake in progress): What did you think of Sam?

Me: Adorable! He says to tell you sorry he missed you yesterday, but will stop by tomorrow—

Henri: Rhett! You nearly stabbed your leg!

Rhett (shrugging, still holding the scissors): Aren't your friends coming up tomorrow?

Me: Down. Yes—on the Metro North train from Poughkeepsie. Jan and Jade. But, Sam said—

Rhett: Don't worry. I'll text Sam. If he comes to visit I'll be discreet about why you're not there—about the library.

(Henri looks at me. I toss a daisy onto the pile, lay down my scissors, and stand.)

Me (looking at my phone): I gotta go. Tim should be out of class by now.

Rhett: Tell Tim I said hi!

(Henri waves her scissors; her dragon feet wiggle.)

2 a.m.: can't sleep.

Tim wondered if Jan and Jade will look up their birth records tomorrow, too, but neither of them was born here. The NYPL only has records for Manhattan, I think. Or all five boroughs? Anyway, I wonder how many other babies—how many Elizabeths—were born in Manhattan my same year on August 18. This could take a while, as I don't really know what to do. Jan says the librarian will help.

Anyway, I reminded Tim that Jan already knows who her birth mother is, just not _where_ she is these days. Jan gets a card now and then, last time from Denver. And Jade—she says such records probably aren't kept in Korean orphanages—but someday she'll find out for sure.

Rhett's keeping all this a secret. She gets how I need to be the one to tell people, _if_ I tell people. (I wish she'd just come out and say she likes Sam and "hands off." You'd think I wouldn't be a threat, since I have Tim.)

Henri told me that her grandmother made her those dragon slippers, to bring her luck and protection at college. Wish I had a pair. It was also Henri's grandmother who named her—not after a male relative, as I figured, but after some fancy women's jewelry and fashion store (where none of us can afford to shop). When I told her that my parents named me Elizabeth Ann not knowing my birth mother had given me the same name, she said, "That's the best story ever! I wish my story was half as good as that. Who wants to be named after a store on Fifth Avenue?"

Cathy's going to like Henri and Rhett. I wish _she_ were coming tomorrow. Cathy's negotiated this emotional landmine already, and might have advice about where to step, where not to.

Oh geez. 2:25 a.m. Make that _today_. I'd just get up and start working on my Alice Munro paper if I weren't so freakin' crazed in the head. I'll say a prayer instead.

Jan & Jade Arrive at GCT
to Stand by Me at the NYPL

At Grand Central I meet Jan and Jade's train.
I spot them right away stepping onto
the platform into the river of heads—I strain

to keep my eye on them until they're so
close we can hug. I feel like a giant,
as I always do, standing there next to

them. I also feel like something else I can't
really name. Neither of them has spent much
time in New York—both their heads are bent

backward; their jaws, open, while they stare at
Grand Central's ceiling made of stars.
My heart feels full, watching them. What

connects us is loss. None of us knows
why our birth mothers gave us up—just that
they did—and now Jan and Jade are here so

I won't have to face alone what today
reveals, or doesn't. As we step out onto
Forty-second Street we zip our jackets, say

all at once how cold it is. Jade and Jan
seem to huddle together as I lead
the way past a coffee and doughnut stand,

newspaper kiosk, and a man who pleads
for spare change on the corner where we wait
to cross Fifth Avenue. Jade mouths, "He needs

help," then turns, gives him forty-eight
cents. As we cross the street, Jan takes Jade's
arm. "No need to protect her—this is a safe

neighborhood," I say. Then my head's a storm
of thoughts; my heart's racing like a subway
train. My face must show a look of alarm—

"Lizzie, everything's going to be okay,"
says Jan, taking my arm now, too. Before
us, the library and its lions loom way

larger than Jade and Jan imagined or
I ever realized. Like the lions, we stare.
"Come on," I say, "What are we waiting for?"

Journal Entry #2173

<u>Scene:</u> **The Milstein Division of United States History, Local History, & Genealogy (NYPL, Room 121)**

Librarian (about mom's age, kind of pretty, caramel-brown hair in a single braid down her back; name tag reads "Sachi"): May I help you find something?

Me: Birth records?

Jan: *Manhattan* birth records.

Librarian (with a glance at Jan's pink hair): What year are you interested in?

Me (blank stare)

Jan: She's a little nervous. (Gives her my birth year, same as hers.)

Librarian: Oh, I'm sorry. Our records only go to 1982.

Jan: *What?*

Librarian: Our records stop—unfortunately—at 1982. The Department of Mental Health kept them for a short while after that, but—

Me: You don't have birth records for anyone born after—

Librarian: 1982.

Jade: Where do you find your record if you were born after that?

Librarian: Well, you can write to Albany for a copy of your birth certificate.

Me: What if your birth certificate doesn't have your birth name? What if it's dated two years after you were born with—a different name?

Librarian (lowering her voice): You're adopted?

Me (my face suddenly hot, I look around before I answer): Yes . . . .

Jan: The guy who runs our Adoption Support Group said anyone born in New York City could find her birth record here.

Librarian: I'm afraid his information is only correct for people born between 1866 and 1982. The State of New York, or your adoption agency, might be able to send you what's called "non-identifying information," but—

Jan: She has that.

Me: From The New York Foundling.

Librarian: I really wish I could help you, girls. But I'm afraid that's all I know.

Jade: Do a lot of adoptees ask you questions like this?

Librarian: Yes, sweetie, they do.

Jan (to me): Let's go.

Me (to librarian): Thanks.

Librarian: Good luck. All three of you.

In a Coffee Shop After Leaving the NYPL

"Well, that was a total waste of time," I
say while Jan and Jade study the menu.
When the waitress comes by, Jan says, "Pie—
apple—and coffee, please. And Jade, you
want the same?" Jade nods. I say, "Make it three,
please," not because I want pie or coffee
but so I'm not odd girl out. The waitress leaves
and Jan says it wasn't a waste, because she
and Jade got to see me, but Joe's got to—
"It wasn't Joe," interrupts Jade. "It was
Sue who found her record there. We assumed—"
"Sue's old," I say. "It's okay," says Jade, "because
you still have one thing you can do." She's smiling.
"Time," she says, "to visit The New York Foundling."

Journal Entry #2174

Scene: Back at Grand Central Terminal

Me: You sure you guys have to leave this early?

Jan: That's okay. The shop's really busy. (Looks at Jade.) We should get back.

Jade: You know I'm helping at the shop now? Not fixing cars—

Me: Yeah, I heard you've been taking business classes. Bookkeeping?

Jan: She answers the phone, makes appointments.

Jade: Part-time until I get my AA.

Me: But the shop is closed tomorrow, isn't it?

Jan: Sorry, Lizzie—Liz—we're gonna miss our train.

Jade: Let us know when you're going to The Foundling!

I walk them down the platform to the Poughkeepsie-bound train. Watch them get on, find a seat. They wave, all smiles, from a window. Part of me wants to go with them. Part of me can't wait to get back to Goddard Hall.

Tim calls, and it's so gorgeous out, I decide to walk back—we talk the whole way.

Dream

No other cars in the school parking lot
except Dad's Subaru. From the front seats
we're counting stars, which begin to fall
from the sky like snow. We should go,
I say as snow-stars blanket the windshield,
start to obliterate the warm glow of the street
lamp we're parked under. "Wait," says Dad.
I pull a parka over my green and white
basketball uniform—knees bare, cold; sneakers
that daring orange. As the car grows dark,
Dad hands me a box I know contains my
silver basketball charm with its inscription
on the back: "Lizzie / My Star." I move to hug
him, but my arms embrace air. He's no longer
there. Now I'm in the driver's seat; Butter's
in the back. *Where's Dad?* I ask the dog, who
only stares ahead, watching snow-stars melt
and slide down glass. Then I know: Dad is dead.

Journal Entry #2175

Walking back from class this morning, the wind nearly blew me over as I rounded the corner of Goddard Hall. So I spent two hours in my room reading Alice Munro's short story "Vandals," glad Rhett was down on the sixth floor. (Debating, she told me later, who was more brilliant: Jane Austen or Charles Dickens. "I'm beginning to believe one cannot be a fan of both," she says, "unless you look to Austen for a glimpse at the concerns of the rich, and Dickens for an understanding of the plight of everyone else.")

By this time I was famished. And in luck. From our hallway window I could tell the trees in the park were barely fluttering, and the sun was out along with a bunch of people on benches not looking like snowmen. I stuffed Ms. Munro into my backpack and headed out, first for a sandwich and then a bench of my own.

Did I hope I'd see R Woman with her guitar? For a second, but I brushed the thought away as my phone chimed like a door bell. Text from Tim.

Him: "Miss u. 70, sunny here"
Me: "Sunnier here. Miss you, too. xo"

Tim says Jade is right: The New York Foundling is next. I almost called there earlier, but the park called to me louder.

Open Secrets

It's still a little cold to be
reading Alice Munro
in the park—too

cold to be reading anything.
But I'm distracted by
her story where

a guy literally loses his
head, and his poor boss has
to pick it up—

while part of me secretly hopes
Guitar/R Woman will
show—so I've claimed

the bench next to her usual
one. It's mid-afternoon
but there are more

squirrels here than people, scampering
about like little kids
on an Easter

egg hunt. I wonder if Munro
actually knew a man
whose head was chopped

off in an accident, and where
squirrels sleep at night. Then there
goes Pigeon Man

with three birds on his shoulders, one
on his head, a dozen
trailing behind

picking at the crumbs he's dropping.
Focus on the story, I think,
but then she's there,

settling on her bench. I try
to pretend I'm into
"Carried Away."

"Let me guess," I hear, *"Cold Mountain?"*
She's glancing from me to
the open book

propped between my mittened hands. "No?
How about *The Ice Queen?*
Or Robert Frost?"

"Frost—I wish," I say. "No, Dante—
'The Inferno.'" We laugh.
"Ah, so that's how

you stay warm out here." She lifts her
guitar from its leather
black case. It's made

of dark wood, like Tim's. "Actually—"
I blurt, "It's an Alice
Munro story."

She looks interested, so I
say, "From her collection,
Open Secrets."

Her large eyes widen. "Now that's some
title. Do you think there
is such a thing

as an open secret?" A jolt
of surprise stabs through my
body. I think,

Where would I begin? "Yes, I do,"
I say at last, and she
nods as if she

agrees. She smiles, then looks away.
For a moment she's still,
then starts to play,

singing, "Secret-keeper, aren't you
tired of locking your heart?
Can't you see all

its secrets tearing you apart?
Toss me that silver key,
let your life start

again, let me set you free . . . " Now
I *am* frozen on this
bench—by her voice,

by those words I know are a song
by Fly, brought on by our
conversation—

so why is my head in a swirl
like I'm in Penn Station
at rush hour?

Late Sunday Morning Surprise

Nothing like a boy at the door
to make a girl suddenly care
what she looks like. Rhett's
still in her torn Ziggy T-Bone
T-shirt and sweats; at least

I'm wearing jeans and one
of Dad's flannel shirts. Rhett's
been teasing me about Tim,
making me laugh 'til it hurts—
since he and I agreed to see

other people, she says, I should
do it (starting with Calvin C.),
stop acting like a nun, and nuns
by the way shave their heads,
and no way will I cut off this mess

of curly locks, much less get out
of bed at 3 a.m. each day to pray...
then there's the knock at our door,
Sam Paris's voice saying he's
the computer repair man. Like

a cat, Rhett springs to her feet,
pounces on her purse, flings some
dirty socks under the bed, swishes
on blush and lipstick, yelling
"Wish you'd called first!" then

unlocks the door with a flourish,
practically taking a bow as Sam
strolls in. This whole production
has so wowed me I've forgotten
to look in the mirror myself. Now

it's too late. "Morning, ladies,"
Sam says, handing us each a mug
of coffee. "You're a prince," Rhett
says as Sam claims her desk chair.
Sam does look like royalty to me,

though his tarnished gold hair
is mussed up. "Thank my roommate
for leaving behind his French press
over break," says Sam. I take a sip—
This'll put hair on your chest, Dad

would have joked. "We were just
talking about Calvin," Rhett tells
Sam, sneaking a peek at me. Sam,
half listening as he reads the spines
of books piled on Rhett's desk, just

says, "Yeah?" Not to be discouraged,
Rhett goes on, "He and Liz have
a lot in common." I feel my right
eyebrow rise. "Like what?" I ask.
Sam looks up, suddenly engaged.

Rhett stares at me, red glasses almost
twinkling. "Smoke's rising from your
ears, you're thinking so hard," I tease.
Sam snickers. Rhett peers thoughtfully
into her mug, says, "You both like old

fogie music, for one. Like what that
woman plays in the park. Our *parents'*
music." I lay my mug on the floor,
sit on Rhett's rug. "Right, or what?"
she pushes. Sam comes to my rescue.

"Speaking of music," he says, "come
hear Minds of Snow—tickets are
cheap! Tonight. In Dumbo." Rhett
says yes as I rise to my feet and
surprise, surprise, say thanks, but no.

Taking Kate to Hear Guitar Woman

Passing under the arch from Washington
Square North is always sort of magical—
I enter the park sensing something special
will happen. Today, I've asked Kate to come
see my dorm, listen to Guitar Woman
if she's here. "Is there some subliminal
message—I sense this has the potential
to be about something more than a social
visit," Kate says. Her thick brown hair is cut
short now that she's head chef at a bistro
called Downtown. I explain I'm just a fan—
then we're close and Ms. R's playing, so
I shut up. I watch Kate's face. "I know what
you mean," she says. "Her voice is like Gram's."

Kate's as practical as an umbrella on a rainy day. She wouldn't stay long to listen to Ms. R (who was singing THE song), but instead wanted to head to my room so she'd have time to meet Rhett and look around before heading to work.

Still, some of the words to that song Ms. R was singing have now become an ear worm—can't get them out of my head:

> Thought I saw you through a window
> one April—there by the gold trees—
> turned out you were me.
> The wind blows
> as though a mother-ghost.
> I was still sea-borne
> and you were my coast.

"Mother-ghost." Does that mean the mother is dead? Just missing? Kate wasn't sure, but she did know it's a song called "When You Never Said Goodbye" by Jessica Rose Hemley. It was a hit when Kate was a freshman in high school.

Kate also said Goddard is one of the nicest dorms she's ever been in—she could see now why I'm in heaven here.

She and Rhett liked each other right away, especially once they realized they're both "foodies." Who knew Rhett watches as many cooking shows as my sister? If they went on about "R.W. Quinn, Master Chef" one more minute, I was going to have to order a pizza.

Kate didn't make a big deal out of Guitar Woman—I was just relieved that when we reached the park, Ms. R had a crowd around her. Kate could see it wasn't just me—lots of people think she's good. And I wasn't implying anything beyond that. What did Kate mean by "subliminal"? She's always reading underneath things; she's an emotional metal detector. Maybe that's why I didn't mention that I plan to call The Foundling soon. She supports my search, but I didn't want to get into another discussion about my reunion fantasies and how I'm always setting myself up for disappointment.

It's so strange, though: I didn't remember how Gram used to sing to us until Kate mentioned it. Gram did have a great voice. That was so long ago! Gram and Mom often sang together. I can remember them harmonizing "New York, New York," kicking up their feet in our living room like the Radio City Music Hall Rockettes.

I haven't heard Mom sing since Dad died, except in church. And that was more of a whisper.

Winter Collage of Days in Washington Square Park

Man wearing a moose suit tells me I'm cute;
jazz band lifts its brass to the smudge of sun, plays
"Nobody Knows Me Better than You"

Troupe of hip-hoppers somersault and flip
for tips to the beat of "Mr. Incognito"
(they've cleared a square of snow for this)

Cocker Spaniel takes its woman for a walk
while she chatters like a squirrel on her phone
(I should talk, the way I can blabber)

Two brown boys run toward the fountain (winter
still, like a painting), pull off their coats. Their mother
shouts, "William! Ephraim! *Bill!*"
(Savory smell wafts from the roasted cashew cart)

A couple kiss under the arch. "Miss!" they call, "Take our picture?"

"That squirrel lady's whacked," says a man walking by to the woman
clutching his arm. "Too warm, but it smells like snow," she replies.
Two squirrels eye her as if she's a snack

In her long, black wool coat, black boots, and black skull cap
R Woman rests a guitar on her lap. Cup of coffee steams
on the bench beside her

A middle-aged guy in an old Army jacket sets a square of cardboard
on a marble bench, then sits on it to read the *Daily News.* He crosses
his legs, reveals snake-skin shoes

Little girl, hair in cornrows with blue and white beads
clutches a thick stump of electric-pink chalk. "Chalk is
for summertime," her father coos

Journal Entry #2177

People think poems that are funny either dishonor the art of poetry ("like posing for a photo next to Michaelangelo's 'David' statue," says Prof. R, "holding your hat over his private parts") or they're just fluff. Professor R's idea seems to be that there are plenty of good, funny poems out there that at the same time are serious and/or say something important. They can make us think, mostly through irony and satire.

There is this old (dead) poet named Theodore Roethke, whose poems I really like. His poem called "Dinky" is hysterical, especially as Prof. R reads it. Sort of a fairy tale, the poem is perfect for little kids. "Dirty Dinky" is a trickster figure, like a leprechaun who casts spells. I thought it was just a nonsense poem, but it turns out it could also be making a dark political statement. Who knew?

Speaking of spells, in class today I mentioned Lucille Clifton's "homage to my hips." My face burned, voice shook, but I recited: "these hips are mighty hips. / these hips are magic hips. / I have known them / to put a spell on a man and / spin him like a top!"

I've been trying to write a funny poem myself. It's harder than I thought. But *all* this poetry stuff is difficult. That's part of the draw—how I lose myself, lose track of time, lose the sense of where I'm sitting, even—as I try to put "best words in the best order," as poet Stephen Dobyns says in his craft book. I keep thinking, keep believing, that if I work hard enough . . . someday, *I'll* write the kind of poems students study in school.

As Winter Term Nears Its End...

"Look who *he's* with," whispers Rhett
as we wander into the cafeteria. "That
Louise is a leech." She's not my favorite

person, either, but I'm not bummed
when Rhett leads us over to Louise
and Sam's table since it's by the window,

meaning views of the park and beyond.
Sam looks relieved to see us, but Louise
looks like she just drank sour milk.

"We're already finished," says Louise
as we sit down. Rhett ignores her, looks
at Sam. "I'm famished." Louise grabs

her empty mug, flits away for more tea
(no way is she not staying). "Well, she's
a snot, as usual," says Rhett. How can

they all sit here and not stare at the park,
all dusted in white from last night's
snow? "Calvin's back," says Sam, who

seems to have noticed me gazing out
the window. "Oh!" Rhett exclaims,
"We'll have to throw a party!"

Did Louise miss the "P" word? Nope.
Already back with her tea, she fakes
enthusiasm. "Good idea!" Rhett's

cheeks match Sam's tomato soup.
"You three spread the word," he says.
"I'll make sure the lounge is free."

Journal Entry #2178

"The term 'famous poet' is a misnomer," said Prof. R, "like 'jumbo shrimp'." It seemed right to end class with everyone laughing. Still, that quote keeps bumping around in my head like a bee caught on a screened-in porch. Really—how many people can name a single poet besides Robert Frost? Okay, so maybe I won't be famous. I just want my poems to be read by more than my family and best friends. [Prof. R was quoting a poet named William Mathews; must look up his work. And oh! How surprised and happy he looked when I asked him to sign my copy of *Redemption Arcade!*]

Prof. James spent our final class comparing Alice Munro with Flannery O'Connor, saying Munro was inspired by O'Connor. Everyone seemed to be nodding as Prof. James said things like, "Where O'Connor's characters seek 'grace' as a gift from God, Munro's characters have a secular vision..." Am I the only ignorant one in the room who hasn't read Flannery O'Connor?! Have I spent too much time reading poetry, not enough reading fiction?!

Anyway, Alice Munro's stories aren't what I'd call "action-packed," even though there are murders and near-murders, drownings and near-drownings. It's all done so *quietly*. But somehow she pulls you in... and there's usually a spooky sense that things aren't going to end well. How does she *do* that? That's what we writers need to study, need to figure out so we can use similar techniques in our own work, says Prof. James. Got to learn how to "read like a writer."

REMINDER: my story's not written by Alice Munro. No more waiting around, hoping to hear from a registry that they've found a "match." This is the time for *action*. Going to the NYPL was like walking into a brick wall. Time to make the call. (Please, God, let *my* story have a happy ending...)

Journal Entry #2179

Appt. with Sophie Fedorowicz
The New York Foundling
Friday, 2 p.m.

So, I did it. I called The Foundling. The social worker who sent me my non-identifying information, Sophie Fedorowicz, seemed to remember me, my "case." She was super nice. My stomach cramps pretty much disappeared as we talked.

Tim thinks Jan and Jade should go with me, but my instincts tell me this time I need to go alone. He finally agreed—"You'll wear your charm, as always . . . I guess that's enough."

I'll tell Kate before I go on Friday. Mom and Bob . . . not sure.

I feel as if I'm about to go skydiving—the plane is in the air; I'm standing at the threshold of an open door, and now I have to jump. Now I have to trust my parachute will open when I do.

Lounge Party to Celebrate
End of Winter Term, Start of Spring

Snowflakes and daisies dangle
from the ceiling; little white
lights frame the room. Aroma
of brownies and sugar cookies
soon wafts past my nose as Henri
slips by with a plate. "Those
don't look like Fig Newtons,"

a boy with an afro jokes. Henri
blows a kiss his way. I'm glad
she doesn't hear him say, "She's
a little fortune cookie! So good
to be back." The party's in full
swing. I should be mingling
like Rhett, who looks stunning

in her gray suede boots, black
tights, short black skirt and gray
sweater. I should be laughing
like Louise, who I admit looks
hot in her tight purple dress,
red hair falling past her hips.
I should be flirting with Calvin,

who is handsome, African
American with stylish gold-
framed glasses and GQ clothes.
I should be meeting all these
people now back for spring
term—Rhett introduced me
to Josh and Fern; through them

I met a girl whose name I forget.
I learn the boy with the afro
is Daryl but goes by Dizzy, turn

to see Sam put his arm around
Rhett. I should take a picture
with my phone, should do so
many things besides drone on

and on in my head, *Lizzie, act
happy . . . stop thinking about
The Foundling.* "Liz!" I hear
Rhett call as I side-step toward
the door. "Come have a drink!"
But I ignore her, slide into the
too-bright light of the hall.

Snow on the first day of spring term apparently means everyone heads to Bobst, the nicest and biggest library I've ever seen next to the NYPL. If the NYPL is a marble palace from the 19th century, then Bobst is a shining glass and brick tower of the 20th. My idea was to head straight from my first class (creative writing workshop) and grab a seat near a window so I could spend some time getting my head around this semester's workload and look out at the park at the same time. Fifty other people had the same idea. But it's warm, and Goddard is close—getting back won't be so hard, though I might be wishing I'd brought my snowshoes.

Spring courses: Writing 2; Cultural Foundations 2 (liberal studies—literature); Social Foundations 2 (philosophy); Creative Writing Workshop: Intro to Fiction & Poetry. Also: Intermediate Spanish.

It felt as if someone had pricked me with a pin when I sat down in workshop. The desk-chairs were arranged in a circle. Louise was right across from me. We spent a lot of energy not looking at each other. I'm much more talkative than she is, and have no idea what to expect from her poems or stories.

Professor Aguero with her wild gray curls is easy-going but totally focused. She has us reading like crazy—"Writers *read*," she says, pacing around the outer circle of our desks as if she's playing Duck Duck Goose. Thanks to her, today I "discovered" Major Jackson and Aracelis Girmay. WOW WOW.

Next week we start bringing in our own work, too. I'm curious about writing some fiction, but Professor Aguero says I can mainly focus on poems if that's my "inclination."

"Focus." It's hard to focus on *anything* for long, except Friday and The Foundling.

———

My idea of heaven: the spring reading series. I'm so psyched, I could kiss my student ID card.

Rhett's Post-Party Blues,
First Day of Spring Classes

Back from the workshop and library, psyched
we're reading Evan Boland and Junot Díaz, I'm
surprised to see Rhett still in bed. "Headache,"
she moans, "Too much vodka, not enough limes."
"Water. You need *water*," I say, grabbing one
from the fridge. She drinks as if her mouth is
a desert. "So, you and sexy Sam Paris had fun
last night," I say as casually as I can. "Oh, *Liz*,"
Rhett moans, "Fun, yeah, but that's it. Another
night of being *friends*." "But he put his arm
around you!" I say, "Rhett, really, any other
girl would take that to mean—" "He put his arm
around me as he told a joke. A freakin' lame
joke. I was a *prop*." "Well, Prop, don't be alarmed,"
I say. "Guess whose red hair burst into flames?"

Journal Entry #2181

By the time I left the library yesterday, it was past noon and the snow had nearly stopped. Rhett was super mad at herself for a) not getting anywhere with Sam ("Maybe he's doing it with a girl back home and just hasn't said," she mused) and b) missing her first two classes, but she recovered enough from her hangover to make her afternoon workshop. We ate peanut butter cookies for lunch, then walked as far as MacDougal Street together. By then there were just a few clouds left; the day had turned bright but colder. Sun glinted off windows of the buildings we passed. Much of the snow was already littered with dirt and the occasional candy wrapper, cigarette butt.

Rhett wanted to know why I left the party so early. I could feel her looking at me intently, listening hard, as I told her about my appointment at The Foundling, just a few days away now. How I'm struggling to focus on school, the search—all the new social stuff sometimes makes me feel like an electrical outlet with too many cords plugged into it—my brain starts to smoke. Rhett slipped her arm though mine before splitting off. "If you need me to go with you, I will—I can," she said. I told her thanks, but no—still, I might need her that afternoon when I get back to our room.

Nearly late to Spanish class, I was relieved to see Calvin sitting in a middle row when I walked in the door. *¡Hola, amiga!* he greeted me, his smile so genuine—a boy-who-doesn't-know-how-handsome-he-is smile—I suddenly saw why Rhett was thinking I'd fall for him.

Spanish Class

It's like being four again,
all the adults around me
jabbering too fast, using big
words I don't know. Or
more like being dropped
in the middle of a foreign
country—in this case,
Puerto Rico—with only
my kindergarten Spanish
to navigate me through
the marketplace, hotel
check-in, restaurants. "*Si,*"
says Senora Arroyo:
"*Hablamos solamente
español en esta clase.*"
We only speak Spanish
in this class. "So," I ask
Calvin, who seems as
stunned by this total
immersion idea as I do,
How do you say—*come
se dice*—'We're doomed'
en español?"

Poetry Reading at the
Lillian Vernon House: Spring Series

(Home of NYU's Creative Writing Program)

If I could only clone myself, be
in a dozen places at once—
every night in New York I could
be a "poetry dork" (Bob's phrase),
hearing writers read their work

downtown, uptown, East Side,
West. One of the best venues is
right here at NYU. Yusef
Komunyakaa read here last week,
and Paul Muldoon. (I swoon just

remembering.) Martha Rhodes,
Sandra Meek, and Robert Hass
are all coming soon. Tonight
it's Jeffrey Harrison, a tall, curly-
haired man not from New York

but Boston. After making a Red
Sox joke to put us all at ease,
he reads "The Fork"—a poem
that makes me laugh so hard
I snort. Of course then I want to

crawl under my folding chair
and die. But everyone else is
roaring, too, so either didn't
hear or don't mind. He then
reads serious poems, many

about his brother who died.
After, at his signing (my cheeks
flush from a glass of wine), I

gush—tell him about my class
with Professor R and how

next week I'll bring "The Fork"
to share with everyone. He gives
me a warm smile, signs my copy
of his book, "To Liz, a young poet
about to take NYC by storm."

Journal Entry #2182

Who ever heard of Insomnia Cookies? Rhett says they got her and Henri though all of last semester. (Chocolate chip delivered warm to Goddard Hall.) I thought she must be kidding. Besides, Rhett could sleep through a rock concert if one happened to start up in our room at 4 a.m. She's a night owl, but she's no insomniac.

I saw Sam and Calvin in the lobby this afternoon, going out as I came in, and they swore she isn't making it up. Sure enough, in the alcove between the outer door of the building and the inner one, there's a stack of flyers—beside one for "20% off at Big B" there's a flyer for Insomnia Cookies.

Sam said, "There's a poem in there somewhere, right, Liz?" "We gotta go," said Calvin, *"Tengo mucho hambre."* Sam looked at me as if I were Calvin's translator. "He's hungry," I explained. "See you both later!"

A poem about cookies sounded odd at first, but Sam got my mind's proverbial wheels turning. Especially since The Foundling appointment is the day after tomorrow, and I'm sleeping like crap.

Insomnia Cookies:
An Advertisement Disguised as a Poem

It is past midnight and you can't sleep?
Have a big test tomorrow, appointments to keep?
Rescue is just a phone call away! A dozen or more
can be delivered right now, warm cookies at your door!
Feel the energy—don't toss and turn like all the rookies—
stay up all night, get things done, with Insomnia Cookies!

Journal Entry #2183

Today's photos from Mom: Butter bounding across our neighbor's field, sporting blue snow boots; Butter asleep on the couch, using a book as a pillow. Want to bet Mom wanted to read that book, but wouldn't wake up the dog? Anyway, he was probably reading it himself through some form of osmosis.

Labrador retrievers don't need snow boots, I told her. But she claims he kept getting ice caught between the pads of his feet, and then he'd lie down and cry because he couldn't bite or lick it out. "Luckily I was there to help each time," she said, "but enough is enough—then I saw the boots at Fur, Fin, & Feather!"

Rhett's from North Carolina and adores snow, because she rarely gets to see it. It does make it hard sometimes for her to go on her (near) daily runs—these days it's either too slippery or too sloppy. No such thing as too cold to run, though, says Rhett. Stick around, I say.

Hanging out in the Sunshine State, Tim is missing out on all this great winter weather. He won't be back north until June from the looks of it, since he's at some tournament (Georgia?) during spring break. How will we make it 'til JUNE?

Odd—he usually calls me in the late afternoon, but I haven't heard from him since breakfast.

Tomorrow: The Foundling, Therefore Tonight: Little Sleep to Be Had

After the first week of classes
I should be sleeping like Rip
Van Winkle, should be keeping
my pillow company. Instead
I'm staring at the clock. School
rocks; I'm happy as a butcher's
dog except mostly I'm thinking
about The Foundling. Why am I
flopping around like a fish
in shallow water? You'd think
I'd been caught in a net, was
about to be someone's lunch.
Reaching for the charm around
my neck, I pray for deep water,
pray for a whole bunch of sleep.

Journal Entry #2184:
Headed to The Foundling in a Few Hours

Kate called: "Got your Dad socks on?" (Yes, and his scarf.)

Tim texted: "Im in ur back pocket." (I wish.)

Jan texted: "Not 2 late! Jade & I could be on next train, arrives 11:42" (I need to go solo on this trip.)

I called Mom. She tried not to act surprised or hurt that I waited this long to tell her where I'm going. I tried to smooth over my guilt by wondering out loud if there's anyone left at The Foundling who might remember her and Dad, how they used to bring pumpkins and apples down for The Foundling kids every fall. She just sighed and said, "Yes, I suppose some of those wonderful women are still there. Good luck, Lizzie."

Then we talked about Butter. He's figured out how to open the refrigerator door. Mom said, "It was cute until it wasn't." (So much for that sirloin she was marinating.)

Bob doesn't know yet.

The New York Foundling: 590 Sixth Avenue, Between Sixteenth & Seventeenth Streets

Just a year and a half ago
Kate and I stood on this
very spot, gazing up
at these twelve brick
stories on Sixth Avenue,
windows all framed in
blue. We had a break-
through that day. Much
of our self-imposed silence
around adoption dropped
away, and she got behind
me on this search. We never
did go in, as I'm about to do.
(We also thought we were
born here—that part wasn't
true; we were brought here
after, before foster care.) Now
no one's carrying me in, no
one's deciding where I'll go
but me. I check my hair
in the glass, take one more
deep breath in the frosty air,
and open The Foundling door.

Sophie Fedorowicz's Small but Sunny Office, The New York Foundling

My life, I think, is lying on that desk.
My first, secret life, hides in that brown folder.
"I'm so glad you came," Sophie says. I smile,
that folder like a sleeping animal between us.

My first, secret life hides in that brown folder.
Sophie says, "I'll help as much as I can."
That folder is a sleeping animal between us.
"You know, by law, I can't tell you everything."

Sophie says, "I'll help as much as I can."
Her gray eyes are kind, look straight into mine.
"You know, by law, I can't tell you everything,
but the letter we sent was missing some details."

Her gray eyes are kind, look straight into mine.
She opens the folder—the animal yawns.
"The letter we sent was missing some details.
Your maternal grandfather was a baker..."

She opens that folder—the animal yawns.
I dig out my pen, start taking notes.
"Your maternal grandfather was a baker;
your maternal grandmother was a nurse..."

I dig out my pen, start taking notes.
My hand shakes—that animal might swallow me whole.
"Your maternal grandmother was a nurse.
She came here to meet with your birth mother."

My hand shakes—that animal might swallow me whole.
"You know you weren't placed for adoption right away.
She came here to meet with your birth mother.
She tried to help your mother make up her mind..."

"You know you weren't placed for adoption right away.
Your grandmother wanted what your birth mother wanted.
She tried to help your mother make up her mind.
Your birth mother wrote a letter. I have it here."

"Your grandmother wanted what your birth mother wanted."
The animal is *mine.* It means me no harm.
"Your birth mother wrote a letter. I have it here.
I'll black out some names, then give you a copy."

The animal's mine. It means me no harm.
Sophie stands, the letter in her hand.
"I'll black out some names, then give you a copy.
It will only take me a few minutes."

Sophie stands, the letter in her hand.
The animal turns its head and winks.
"It will only take me a few minutes—"
She leaves me and that folder alone.

The animal turns its head and winks.
It's now or never, the animal whispers.
She's left me and that folder alone.
Just a sneak peek, it says. *Quick! Do it now!*

It's now or never! the animal whispers.
I hesitate—Sophie, she trusts me—
Just a sneak peek, it says. *Quick! Do it now!*
I leap to my feet, flip open the folder.

I hesitate—Sophie, she trusts me—
but this is my chance; I have to take it.
I leap to my feet, flip open the folder.
There it is! My name. Elizabeth Ann Smith.

This is my chance; I have to take it.
I think I hear Sophie coming back.
There it is! My name. Elizabeth Ann Smith.
I sit back down, try to take that in.

* 93

I think I hear Sophie coming back.
Holy shit. I think I know my real name.
I sit back down, try to take that in.
Now here's Sophie. "Sorry that took so long."

Holy shit. I think I know my real name.
Smith. Smith? Oh *geez*—could that be for real?
Now here's Sophie. "Sorry that took so long."
She hands me the letter. "Read this at home."

Smith. *Smith?* Oh geez—could that be for real?
How many Smiths live in Manhattan alone?
She hands me the letter. "Read this at home.
Your birth mother loved you very much, Lizzie."

How many Smiths live in Manhattan alone?
"I'm so glad you came," Sophie says. I smile.
Your birth mother loved you very much, Lizzie."
My life, I think, is lying on that desk.

Post-Foundling Fall-Out

I. Live Letter in My Backpack

Instinctively I walk toward home, toward
Goddard, when I leave The Foundling—over
to Fifth Avenue, then down to where it ends,
emptying out at Washington Square Park
like a river empties itself into the sea.

The letter seems to breathe, that animal now
inside my backpack. *Not here, don't read it
here,* I think, staring at the stone arch.
My legs feel heavy, as if I've been wading
through water. Any minute, I fear, something's

going to break—something's going to come
spilling down Fifth Avenue like a tidal wave
and take me with it, tumbling and gasping.
It's then that the idea comes, like a voice
outside myself. (That animal?) I turn right,

follow Waverly Place a couple of blocks
to Sixth Avenue, turn left, and here it is:
Saint Joseph's Church. St. Joseph, Patron
Saint of Families. (How did I know that?
Dad. *Dad!*) Inside, noise from the street

shuts off like a radio. Smell of candles,
wood, the cold that clings to my coat calms
me. Streams of light filter through stained
glass windows. It all feels familiar, right.
Here is sanctuary, my safe place to read

a letter from my first mother. A woman
I knew once. Her voice, her heartbeat,
her every movement made up my world.
How is it possible she's a stranger now?
How could she do it—say goodbye, pull

away... *forever?* Kneeling in the back pew,
I try to pray. I'm frozen. *Oh, Dad,* I say,
Pray for me. I can't right now. I sit back.
Breathe. Stare at the altar, dimly lit. Then
open my backpack. Pull out the letter. Read.

THE LETTER

(In elegant handwriting. All references to my name, my birth mother's
name, and the social worker she addressed it to are blacked out.)

Dear ███████

When you asked me to write a letter expressing my hopes and wishes for
███████████ future and adoptive home, my mind filled immediately with
so many thoughts. I'll try to list them here, selecting the most crucial else
I'll go on forever. Or else words will begin to fail me.

Naturally, a loving home where there are deep religious convictions
is very desirable. One also where education—formal and self-education
through reading, etc.—plays a central role every day. So many doors are
open to the mind that is filled with the beauty to be found everywhere—
in nature, poetry, music. The person who is out to learn all that is good
sees so much more in everyday life, and lives a much richer existence
than the one who remains passive in the doldrums of routine.

███████████, no doubt, has been blessed with a love of music, since it is
a strong family characteristic. I have been fortunate in having had voice
lessons (and even had a role in a college play) and piano lessons, and my
appreciation for accomplished musicians is great. I do hope that music
will somehow be part of her life.

As for brothers and sisters—definitely there should be some—
preferably a brother three to six years older and a sister a year ahead or
behind. One more brother or sister younger would be nice also. To me

that gives her the protection of a big brother, the companionship of a sister close in age, and another child to ward off anyone's being spoiled.

My admiration for the teaching profession is great, and since I plan to be a teacher, I would hope that either one of the adopting couple be in the educational field. Oh, how I'd love to guide her myself! Knowing she is in a home similar to what I would want to give her will be of much consolation.

As for nationality/background, to me the generous nature and "get-aheadness" of the American is a proud heritage. In other words, this isn't a concern if my other hopes are fulfilled.

Please don't let her grow up in the city. This writer has always loved the country life where she grew up, even though she's had a few years' taste of the "big city."

There is so much more that could be said, but I realize I must put my trust in you and the other people there who, I know, have ███████ best interest at heart.

I'm to sign the papers on Friday. Dear God, how will I do it! Never could I have dreamed of such mental and heartfelt torment. It cannot be described.

Be assured, ██████, that you and your colleagues will remain in my prayers.

Gratefully,

████████████████

II. Oh, Mother—

Oh mother of wishes, mother
of prayer. Teacher-mother.
Wise mother. Mother of music,
nature, *poetry*. Tormented
mother. Thoughtful mother.
Mother who hesitated. Mother
who surrendered. Mother,
it didn't have to be like this. All
I ever wanted was to know you
loved me. That you hadn't
forgotten me. Mother, I will find
you. Mother, you want me to
find you. I know that now. God
knows that. *God? Please help me.*

III. It Hits Me

Trudging down the steps and out
of the church, wandering west,
I reach the river. The Hudson, my
river that runs by New Hook
and feels like home. Here there
are benches but few people. Too
cold. Perfect for thinking. For re-
reading. Laughing to myself a bit
crazily, *No doldrums of routine*
in this girl's life. Then it hits me
like Gram's big old brick of
a Manhattan phone book: Smith.
I was Elizabeth Ann *Smith.*

Journal Entry #2185

By the time I left the river and got back to the dorm, it was dark. Rhett was waiting on her bed, just opening a fat book—*Middlemarch*. The George Eliot book she couldn't wait to begin once she learned it was assigned in her Victorian Novel class. When she saw me walk in, her flash of smile changed to a "I'm-concerned-and-here-if-you-need-me" look.

"I'm okay," I said, then slipped behind the wall between our desks and stared down at my bed. Gram's patchwork quilt, baby-chick yellow and cornflower blue, looked so comforting. *She's keeping an eye on you, too, right alongside Dad,* I thought. Instead of sliding underneath, I lay on top of its once-bright squares, hands at my sides feeling its worn softness. Gazing over at my desk, at my laptop, my pile of books, I thought, *Tomorrow.* Then I rolled over and fell asleep without even taking off my coat.

It was 1 a.m. when I woke 45 minutes ago. A mess of texts and a voicemail from Mom wait in my phone. I'll respond tomorrow. (Mom's probably a nut case. Damn, I should have called her—but just . . . couldn't.) After I undressed & put on my sweats, I peeked around our wall—Rhett was out. I ran into our bathroom, brushed my teeth, realized I was hungry. Thank goodness for those brownies Mom sent. Brownies and Diet Coke: the dinner of champions. I brushed my teeth again, dived back into bed with this journal.

Rhett just came in. I told her I'll talk with her tomorrow, that right now I just need to sleep.

No one needs to know I have that letter, I've decided. She wrote it for me.

Poetry. She wrote the word *poetry*.

Rhett Says, Go See Your Sister, So I Call Kate

Kate's between roommates so I have a key
to her second-floor walk-up on Avenue B.
As soon as I step in the door she looks at me
and says, "I'll make us some tea." That means,
Let's talk. Unlike Mom or Bob, Kate always
asks, "Hear anything from the registries?"
Then says, "Wait. Be patient," when I tell her
No. But today we sit on her couch and she says,
"You have news." I do! My tea is cold
by the time I've told her about everything
but the letter. (Would it make Kate wonder
if *her* birth mother loves *her?*) We blow
our noses, wipe our eyes. I know it would
be a lie to think this isn't hard on Kate,
too. I touch her arm. "You are the best
sister," I say, "I wish—" but she stops me.
"Shush. You'll make me cry again." Kate
makes another cup of tea for herself, warms
mine up in the microwave. "Smith is such
a crazy twist," she says. "But I know how
to save you some anxiety. Let's call Mom.
No—I'm not out of my mind! She'll be fine."

I Call Mom from Kate's Apartment

As if I'm the mother and she, the adopted child;
as if she's made of delicate china and might
chip, I'm gentle, take my time telling Mom
about my visit to The Foundling. First I focus
on the building ("It hasn't changed!" she said
and sighed); then Sophie's kindness—how
she came down to the lobby with me to say goodbye, how she said I could call her anytime,
how she said how blessed I am to have such
a great family. Mom ate that up. When she didn't
press for more details, I knew Mom's emotional
cup was full—we'll get to those later. I could tell
she was crying after I said I loved her—that's
when I heard the whine: so was Butter. "Hey,
you were right," I tell Kate. "Everything *is*
fine. Butter just needs his own supply of tissues."

Journal Entry #2186

<u>Scene:</u> **I call Jan and tell her what happened at The Foundling**

Jan: That ROCKS! You totally did it, Liz! You beat the freakin' system!

(Muffled joyful cries in background.)

Me: Is that Jade?

Jan: Yeah, let me put you on speaker phone.

Jade: Lizzie! You know your birth name!

Me: You two—it's great, but don't you get it? My last name is Smith. Like, you ever heard of the proverbial needle in a haystack?

Jan (hesitates): Well, there's *that*—

Jade: It's like having Kim as a last name in Korea.

Me: Rhett says it's like finding a certain grain of sand in the Sahara desert.

(Silence.)

Jade: Okay, you still have one thing you can do.

Me: What?

Jan: Call Joe?

Jade: Exactly.

———

I call Tim when he gets out of class. His first question when I finish my story is, "How are you feeling? Are you okay with all this?" It almost makes me tell him about the letter—but I don't. (I might have read it more times now than I've read my non-identifying letter that The Foundling sent me last year. . . a zillion times plus one.)

Tim says he read a story about two sisters—one adopted—who found each other on Facebook. He'll send me the link. But about "Smith" he said, "That's messed up. I'm so sorry, Liz. I mean, could it be any worse?"

I did spend a few hours online again, searching. Forget that. Jade's right— the support group met last night, so I know Joe's back from his trip. I'll call him. In a day or two.

Text from Bob: "Ms. Smith: Kate called. Worried for ur heart & dont want it broken. But do what u have to do. Maybe this summer u'll come to CA. Lots of Smiths here. Meanwhile, study hard. Love u."

Not sure if this was supposed to make me laugh, but it did—before it made me cry.

I think my birth mother would be (will be?) happy to know—The Foundling couldn't have found me a better family. I mean, she almost describes the McLanes "to the letter" in her letter.

———

Text from Jan: "Call Joe yet?"

I text back: "Too busy. Soon."

What I don't say: My heart's a runaway horse that my mind keeps whipping from behind. I just need to STOP for a few days before I make another move in this search. Catch my breath. Absorb *Smith* . . .

Birth Name Villanelle

Anyone asks how I know, I'll plead the fifth—
I think I did what anyone would do.
What's worse than learning your birth name is Smith?

I'm not going to feel all guilty over this.
I just took what was mine—that much is true.
Anyone asks how I know, I'll plead the fifth.

It does no good to ask "What if—"
but couldn't my name have been Crane or Drew?
What's worse than learning your birth name is Smith?

Sophie didn't smell trouble—not even a whiff.
She left the folder—maybe she wanted me to—?
Anyone asks how I know, I'll plead the fifth.

My name could have been Frost, or Hall, or Jiff
like the peanut butter. Even *Jones* would do.
What's worse than learning your birth name is Smith?

Hardly any words even rhyme with Smith!
I'm bummed it doesn't sound more Scottish, too.
Anyone asks how I know, I'll plead the fifth.
What's worse than learning your birth name is *Smith?*

Old Habits Die Hard

Still, I stare. I don't mean to.
But I ponder women's faces
on the subway, on the street,
standing on line at the coffee
shop, post office, bus stop,
deli. It doesn't die easily, this
lifelong obsession with finding
someone who looks like me.
When I moved to the city,
I thought, *Here I'll really have
a chance.* But now that hope
has collapsed like a balloon
slashed by a knife disguised
as a sentence: "This writer
has always loved the country life."

Ruth

After my morning class,
after talking with Tim
while gulping down eggs
in the cafeteria, after
spending four hours
studying in the library,
I treat myself to coffee
in the park. Ms. R hasn't
been around all week—
I've been dying to speak
with her, learn her name.
So I'm psyched she's here,
though she's claimed "my"
bench—a smoochy couple
sits on hers. I'd like to ask
them to move . . . then they
do. A sign, I think. Maybe
my luck's improving. Ms. R
plucks a string on her guitar,
winces, adjusts a little peg
at the top of the wood neck,
plucks again. Her black
wool hat makes her face look
paler—that face, those huge
brown eyes, now look at me.
I've been staring. Again.
"Hey," she says, "No book
today?" My cheeks feel
warmer than my coffee cup.
Pointing to my backpack,
I say, "Plenty." She almost
smiles, gazes up at the bare
trees. "A Thomas Hardy
kind of day, all this late
winter gloom," she says.
I confess I haven't read

him yet, though my room-
mate Rhett raves about his
book—*Tess,* something.
"Tell you the truth," she says,
I've only read his poems.
And by the way, I'm Ruth."
My cup nearly slips from
my hand. "Liz," I manage
to say. She smiles for real,
says, "Don't be so impressed,
Liz—I read Hardy in college
because I had to. But I do like
poetry. It's like music—all
about rhythm and emotion."
"Me, too," I stammer—"I'm
studying it at NYU—" then
my head's a muddle; my
coffee's a puddle at my feet.
Ruth pretends not to notice,
goes back to tuning her
guitar. *You're over-reacting,*
Lizzie McLane, I scold myself.
Yes, yes, you are.

Journal Entry #2188

Am I drawn to Ruth's playing—even drawn to Tim's—because, as my birth mother says, I'm basically born to appreciate music? It's in my blood, right? After all, in fourth grade I showed up for my first guitar lesson. The rented guitar's neck was in my right hand; its body was held with my left arm. "That's how a lefty plays," said Mr. Viani. "Yes, I'm a lefty," I said. "Well, you can't play that way. You have to play this way," he said, holding his guitar as a mirror image to how I held mine. When I said no way, so did he. Dad and Mom wouldn't make him teach me left-handed, suggested I take flute instead. But I wanted to play guitar. I guess I still do. Maybe I'm playing out my guitar fantasy through Tim and now Ruth.

I don't know anyone who plays piano, but I love that sound, too. Not just guitar. All music, all instruments. Hey, I even like the accordion. Sometimes.

And sing? Can I sing? I sing in the car, in the shower, down at the river and on the hiking trail around Rothenberg's Pond. Back in high school, Cathy and I used to harmonize "Don't Step on My Shadow," and I loved to croon along with Dad when he sang "Mrs. Murphy's Chowder." But that doesn't mean I have a good voice like him and Gram. Maybe it's not bad. Maybe voice lessons . . . like *she* had.

So what, Ruth likes poetry. Lots of people like poetry. Lots.

Birth Mother

You were stories
I told myself:
"Once upon a time
there was an artist,
a beautiful woman,
a lost woman, a woman
of intelligence, of
integrity, of guilt
who carried me
inside herself until
I was ready to be
in the world. Then
she gave me away
like another painting,
another song—
a sacrifice to her muse—
a symbol of sorrow,
of mastery, of love
because she was poor,
because she was famous,
because she loved
the life she had before
she created me. But
these stories were
only my daydreams,
my art, my mirrors.
Now the true story is
stepping off the stage,
off the page—each
letter formed by her
hand a little ladder
for me to climb toward
truth. I'm rising rung
by rung, first mother.
I'm reaching for your
hand. Let there be

no more anguish, no
more shame, mother.
Throw me down
a light. Throw me
down your name.

Bad Dream as Haiku

Ruth's behind Sophie's
desk, saying, *"She loved you so
much, she gave you up."*

Rhett's Anti-Bad Dream Prescription

I wake shaking—call
Rhett's name. She's already
peeking around our
little wall. "Another
bad dream?" she whispers,
then sits on the end of
my bed. "The same dream,
different version," I say,
nodding my head. "This
time it was Ruth, not Mom.
It felt like a *sign,* trying
to tell me that—that we'll
never—that she won't—"

"A diversion! *That's*
what you need! Let's go
bowling at that place
on the river," she says,
"just us girls, you and me
and Henri." Calling Joe
can wait another day
or three. Rhett gleans
from my smile that I'm
powerless—can't say
no. Next I know she's
running for the bathroom:
"Dibs on the shower!"

No Fun (Even Though I Let
Rhett Win at Bowling Yesterday)

"You are *no fun,* Liz McLane," Rhett says as I stuff
dirty clothes into a basket. She's sitting cross-
legged on her bed; Sam's in her chair, feet propped
on her desk. "Liz spent all morning at the library
and now she's doing laundry!" she complains to Sam.
"Come have lunch with us first," he says. "Your favorite
place on St. Mark's—" I hold up a bottle of detergent
as if it's a stop sign. "Don't tempt me," I say, tossing
the bottle in the basket, then sneaking a peek at Rhett.
I'm sure she doesn't want me tagging along when she
has Sam to herself. "Calvin's coming, too," she says,
"and maybe Henri. Just the diversion you need!"
Resolute, I place a book of poems next to the detergent.
"Marilyn Nelson's coming with me to the laundry room,"
I say, "but call if you go to The Rock." When I open
the door, Henri is there, a plate of cookies in her hand.
"Save one of those for me, or you're all in trouble,"
I call over my shoulder as I head down the hall. "No
guarantees!" says Henri. "Party pooper!" calls Rhett.

Journal Entry #2189:
Killer Chocolate (ex-lax) Cookies

What's with it with girls? Are boys ever this mean? I thought I'd seen it all between Stella and Gabby at SU—but this nearly tops them:

I'm just about to walk into the laundry room when I hear a voice talking real low, and then hysterical laughter. Louise and her roommate, Kimiko. So I stop to listen, hear: "Stupid Henri's on her way right now! I hope Rhett's a total pig and eats the whole plate."

I tip-toe backwards to the elevator and shoot back to our room as quick as I can. Too late—Rhett, Sam, Henri, and Calvin (who'd shown up right after I left) have *all* eaten the cookies but three, which they've saved for me. When I tell them what I'd overheard, they look at each other as if I'd said they were all under arrest. Henri said she did think it strange when Louise asked her to bring the cookies upstairs, but figured it was some kind of peace offering. (Little does Sam know they're basically fighting over *him.*) Who would have guessed they were laced with ex-lax, what grandmothers take when they need to . . . "go"?! "They did taste kind of weird," said Calvin, his dark eyebrows drawn down with worry.

It only took half an hour. First, Henri looked like she was in a horror movie—the zombies had just broken down our door. She didn't say a word, just fled. Next, Calvin, who normally moves like a dancer, ran out like an Olympic track star with a bad back. Sam looked surprised, like someone told him his head was on fire, and fled after Calvin. It wasn't a pretty sight. Rhett was in our bathroom so long, I had to knock on Marion and Suzanne's door and ask to use theirs.

The best revenge, I told Rhett, is the fact that Sam ate them, too—Louise will want to die when she hears that. But I have the feeling that revenge won't stop there.

Well, Rhett did say I need a diversion. Beyond bowling, that is. And since I can't head to Florida (what a dream of a diversion THAT would be), I have an idea.

Postcard from Mexico

*Dear Lizzie—I'm still absorbing all you told me
in your last letter. (Shouldn't you be studying
instead of writing 10-pg. letters in the library?!
Not that I'm complaining, or trying to sound
like your mother.) Smith is a great name. Your
people back in Scotland were probably blacksmiths,
right? Cool. Still, I know your head's spinning.
That's how mine was. These searches, these
birth parents, do a number on you. Maybe you
should wait to call Joe about the next step, focus
on school 'til summer? Then I'll be there, too!
Just a thought. Here, I'm trying to break it to
the kids that I'm leaving them. It's only by
promising to come back that I can get them
to settle down. How I wish I could take them all
home! (Well, most of them. LOL) Hang in there,*
mi amiga. Este verano vamos a hablar español
juntas, si? *Don't drop that class!*

Love,
Cathy

Revenge Is Powdery White

Four a.m. is the time to strike, while your enemy's sleeping.
(It's a trick your sister knew, a harmless pain-in-the-butt.)
After, you'll hope the war is done, though careful watch you'll be keeping.

Henri's door is across from hers—from there Rhett will be creeping.
(With her hair dryer, extension cord—that Rhett, she's got guts.)
Four a.m. is the time to strike, while your enemy's sleeping.

Along the floor below that door, Rhett sprinkles powder till it's heaping.
(Calvin and Sam are ready to run, grinning like two nuts.)
After, you'll hope the war is done, though careful watch you'll be keeping.

There's one moment of near-panic: Sam's fancy phone starts beeping.
(He runs into Henri's closet, behind him the door's quick-shut.)
Four a.m.'s the time to strike, while your enemy's sleeping.

Rhett turns on the dryer, blows powder, so under the door it's seeping—
then blasting white into Louise's room—that place is turned Eskimo hut.
Now you hope the war is done, though careful watch you'll be keeping.

Louise and Kimiko are now awake—you can hear them weeping.
You and your friends are running fast, laughing like you don't know what.
Four a.m.'s the time to strike, while your enemy's sleeping.
Now you hope the war is done, though careful watch you'll be keeping!

Henri's Post-Operation Baby Powder Report

After a bomb blast, when everything and everyone
is covered in dust—that's what it looked like
when Louise opened her door. Odor of baby powder
crept into the hall. All was white—floor, beds, desks,
books, shoes, Kimiko and Louise—except for the brown
and pink streaks running down their cheeks. Louise
looked like a rabbit, Henri says, and seemed to admit
defeat. "Everyone hates me!" she shrieked, then
slammed her door shut, shooting a puff of powder
into the air. "All's fair in love and war," I remind
Henri, giving her a squeeze. But from the look on her
face it's clear she feels sorry for Kimiko and Louise.

When My Birth Mother Said Goodbye

They might have let her
dress me one last time—

something yellow, my
favorite color; something

as soft as a heart that is
breaking. She might have

smothered me with kisses,
an aching mother's desperate

breath unable to stop time's
flames from engulfing us.

When I try to imagine—
remember that day, that last

moment, the final kiss—it's
as if an invisible hand pulls

me back from a dark,
bottomless abyss

Journal Entry #2190: Like People Who've Been Through Some Kind of Trial Together

... an ice storm that knocks out power in a little town for weeks, or a broken elevator that traps its occupants for twenty-four hours, or some crazy bomb threat that keeps people locked down in their dorm for a few days—the Fake Insomnia Cookie Incident and resulting Operation Baby Powder has brought our little group closer. Sam, Calvin, Henri, Rhett, and I hang out all the time now—in our rooms, on the third floor, and often during lunch or dinner. Louise avoids us as if we've got the chicken pox (or as if, says Sam, we're Red Sox fans). So does Kimiko, who was in on the making of those cookies. We all just hope this "food fight" doesn't go another round. It's hardest for Henri, living across the hall from them—but she says it inspired her to diet. She's already lost five pounds!

Speaking of sports: Rhett ran track, swam in high school. All individual sports. She doesn't "get" basketball like Sam and Calvin do. When we start talking Syracuse vs. Georgetown, she suggests we all go out for a drink. She knows how to steal those boys' attention. But if it's early enough, we go to The Rock—and talk basketball.

Meanwhile, Rhett's taking secret photos of Sam with her phone. She has 19 so far. Sam wielding a charcoal pencil like a pointer as he talks; Sam watching Calvin flex his muscles; Sam drinking a Coors straight from the bottle. She does have a few "authorized" photos too, including one I took of her, Henri, Calvin, and Sam outside the Museum of Natural History. Plus a lady in Central Park took a photo of the five of us beside the John Lennon "Imagine" memorial. (All of our parents are Beatles fans.)

Writing that last paragraph, I realized something. Sam has the most unusual scent, which I just can't seem to place. Until now. *Pencils.* He smells like graphite. Like my Mirado Black Warrior #2s! (Never want to be caught without one, in case the muse pays me a visit.) No wonder I like Sam so much. But not like Tim. Tim's scent is Irish Spring soap and green sunshine ...

Gotta stop thinking about Tim, about calling Joe (soon)—and read about Copernicus.

Torn

This is such a bad time to search for my mother.
My grades will suffer—I should focus on school.
My body's in one place, my mind in another.

I'm writing an essay on Heaney's "The Otter,"
then find myself staring into space like a fool.
This is such a bad time to search for my mother.

Studying Spanish verbs, my thoughts start to wander.
The professor calls on me—what's "dunce" in *español?*
My body's in one place, my mind in another.

Tim says all will be fine. I'm beginning to wonder.
Should I keep going or wait? My heart's in a duel.
This is such a bad time to search for my mother.

Today it started to rain. I ran for cover—
a taxi just missed me! I would have been gruel.
My body's in one place, my mind in another.

But this is my chance—I might not get another.
If I wait, she could die. Life can be that cruel.
This is such a bad time to search for my mother—
my body's in one place, my mind in another.

I feel like a hunter chasing some last-of-its kind animal, or even something magical—a unicorn—and if I pause too long to rest, it will escape me forever. So I spent all night on the phone with Tim and Kate. I almost called Jan, but by then it was after midnight. She's in bed by 10. Besides, Jan gets all riled up when we talk about the search, and I didn't have the energy to deal with that.

Talking with Tim helps most. He doesn't give me advice. Doesn't try to "fix" things (as if he could). He listens. Then he says things like, "It's as if you've been a ship at sea all of your life. You keep looking for land, and sometimes you see a sign—a raven with a twig in its beak, a column of smoke far off in the distance—but the moment you think you're close to a port, a storm whips up and turns you all around and the clues disappear." *"Yes! That's it,"* I say. And he says, "Just remember—I'm here, with you on deck. And this ship will find what it's looking for. We just gotta keep our eyes on the horizon."

Kate's mostly worried, as I know Mom is, about how all this is affecting me and, by extension, my school work. Being in the library—seeing everyone studying—inspires me, helps me concentrate. So does listening to classical music. Who knew? Of all people, *Bob* suggested that.

Rhett says she feels like a newcomer to this story and can't really give an opinion, but wants to support me whatever I do. Thank goodness I have such a fabulous roommate. I really want to talk with Henri, Calvin, and Sam, too—they don't know about all this. Yet. It's just so...BIG. So—personal.

Rhett did put her stellar roommate status to a small test, asking if we could move all of my poetry books to *her* side of the room. "Since Sam spends so much time looking at them while he's here..." she tried, then quickly added, "Kidding!" I must have had my mama bear face on. Those books are my cubs.

"I didn't have my heart set on your approbation," Rhett said with a sly smile. That girl spends too much time living in the 19th century.

Journal Entry #2192:
Tim's Valentine's Day Card

Zombies are dead,
my avatar's blue,
martinis are neat,
and so are you.

Thought this card would make you laugh. I don't have an avatar, though, so for the poet in you, I wrote two alternative second lines:

only drummers sniff glue

or

my cat has the flu.

Maybe I should start writing greeting cards, huh?

Miss you.

Love,
Tim

The card *did* make me laugh, but the dozen yellow roses that came with it—well, I must have looked like a proud princess carrying those up from the lobby. Our room smells like summer. Like Gram's house—she always had fresh roses in her kitchen.

———

Reached into my backpack a few minutes ago, thinking I'd call Joe—but left my phone where it was.

This week. I'll call him by Wednesday at the latest.

Finding Our Places

We're all on our way to Klong for lunch—
Henri and I walk side by side while ahead
of us Rhett strolls between Sam and Calvin.
Henri's telling me about Chinese New Year—
she's a dragon and there won't be another
dragon year until 2024. She says something
about luck and the color red, but I'm studying
her flushed face from the corner of my eye,
thinking, *She thinks Rhett's the lucky one
right now.* Calvin keeps extending his left
arm behind Rhett's back without quite
touching her, as if he's afraid she'll fall.
Back on Eighth Street, Sam did slip on
some ice, but caught himself. Now we're
all at Astor Place—the three of them dash
across Fourth Avenue, leaving Henri and me
on the island near the subway station, its
glass and cast-iron kiosk always so alluring—
makes me want to climb down and ride
the 6 train just for the thrill. "Calvin's
such a gentleman," sighs Henri, all googly-
eyed. Our friends wait for traffic to pass,
so we can join them. "He's a total sweet-
heart," I agree, wondering why I hadn't
realized until now that Henri's fallen for
Calvin. "He probably thinks I'm as cute
as a Chinese dumpling, only not as
appetizing," she says. How to respond?
As we cross the street, I say, "He's not
shallow like that—" but then we're within
earshot, and Rhett's saying she's starving,
as in hurry up. At Klong I try to maneuver
so Henri's next to Calvin, but somehow he
winds up next to Rhett and across from Sam;
Henri's next to Sam and across from Rhett,
and I'm on the table's end, with Calvin to my

left, Sam to my right. Lucky me, I guess.

(See diagram:)

```
              C    R
       L
              S    H
```

In Workshop Today

"A theater with no actors, no musicians"—
that's how Louise's poem titled "Home" begins.
As she reads it to our class, she twirls one long red
strand of hair around her finger—its nail, all nails
on both hands chewed down and nearly bleeding. Silence
hovers in the air like mist when she's finished. "This
is a wonderful example," says Professor
Aguero at last, "of poem as metaphor . . ."
After her comments, everyone in class seems to
have something to say—some offer suggestions, but
most simply praise the lines they like. Stunned, I realize
it's my turn. I stare at the poem in my hand.
"I agree the last line is totally earned," I
begin—"that image of the curtain made of glass . . ."
I look up. Louise, watching me, seems ready to
bolt out the door. But I continue, "I might take
out the line that begins 'Trees glisten'—it's the one
place she mixes metaphors—but mainly I want
to say, this is a poem I wish I'd written."

Journal Entry #2193

Scene: I call Joe Alley, director of adoption support group, Stone Falls, NY

Joe remembers me: "Yes, of course, Lizzie—you're friends with Jade and Jan. Went off to Syracuse University last fall, right?"

I quickly explain where I am now and get to the real subject. After I describe how Jan & Jade & I bombed at the NYPL, I tell him about my visit with Sophie at The Foundling.

Then:

Me: So, my birth name is Smith.

Joe (hesitates): Smith?

Me: Smith.

(He doesn't ask me how I found this out. I'm glad. But he hesitates again.)

Joe: Lizzie, I know you've been thinking about this search for a long time—and I think you're as ready now as you'll ever be to discover—well, whatever you'll discover. But with a last name like Smith—you need a private investigator.

Me: You mean a private eye? Like on TV?

Joe: This woman—she has one guy, Jim, I think, who works with her—she's the best at this. And you can trust her. She's a birth mother who found her own child. Her firm is called Kin Solvers. You won't find her listed anywhere—if you do this, you have to be aware it's not legal in New York State.

Me: Not legal.

Joe: I know. It's not fair. This is your mother—your *birth* mother. *Your* life.

But until they change the laws—let me give you Karen Mason's phone number. Then talk with your parents before you call, okay? At least, I have to suggest that.

I don't correct him—"parent." Singular. But I do write down the number.

Pulling Back

As soon as I hear Tim's voice—usually
so calm, so *suave*—I know something's wrong.
Or weird. "How's everyone getting along
post Operation Baby Powder?" he
wants to know. I tell him about Louise's
poem in workshop, how we walked to the dorm
together afterward, and might have formed
not quite a friendship, but a peace treaty,
a mutual respect. I get the sense
Tim isn't listening. "Remember how
we said we'd date other people?" A tense
silence follows his question. Then, POW—
it hits me. I want to ask, "What's the wench's
name?" Instead I say, "Now? Really, Tim? *Now?*"

Journal Entry #2194

<u>Scene:</u> **The rest of the damned phone conversation**

I'm thinking: *"Zeena"?* Is that a real name? I guess it's actually Evelina. She's from the Philippines and sounds very perky. And pretty. Plays golf. I'm doomed.

Tim: I'm still your best friend.

Silence. I have no answer for that. And no way am I telling him about my call to Joe Alley.

Tim: How else will we know if we don't date other people?

Me: Know what?

Tim: Don't be mean.

Me (my throat feels tight . . . can't help crying): It's just—bad timing.

Tim: Lizzie, I'm *here* for you! *Always!*

Me: I gotta go. But—okay.

Tim: Okay? Call you later?

Me: Tomorrow. Maybe.

Tim: I'll call you tomorrow. Promise.

Me: No need to promise.

Rhett's in class.
Henri's on some kind of outing to MoMA.
Heading down to Sam & Calvin's room.

As Gram Used to Say, "A Friend in Need Is a Friend Indeed"

Who's standing there when the elevator opens
on the third floor but Sam. He takes one look
at me, reaches out a hand, and I'm sobbing
in his arms. His graphite pencil smell calms me
for a second, but then I think of Tim's arms—
and I'm a mess again. Sam puts one arm around
my shoulders, leads me to his room. "Don't you
have class?" I manage to ask. "Yeah, soon—
but it's close by," he says. "Besides, leaving you
like this is the last thing I'll do." Sam's side
of the room looks like a hurricane hit—sketch pads,
socks, charcoal pencils, books, and tubes of paint
everywhere. I collapse in Calvin's chair. Sam
sits on Calvin's bed, says, "You okay, Liz?
Is it Tim?" And I start to sob all over again.

A Very Long Night

(Back in my room)

It reminds me of last summer—looking in the mirror,
barely recognizing the girl I see—only this time,
I *like* the me who's standing there, black mascara
running down her cheeks. By the time I've made
myself look as normal as possible (my puffy eyes
make my face fish-like, despite all make-up tweaks),
Rhett is back. I thought she'd say Tim's news just
makes me free to date Calvin, but she sees how
upset I am. Besides, she knows in my mind, no boy
stacks up close to Tim. More than that, she knows
I'm planning to call Kin Solvers—I didn't need this
blow. "How could he? . . . *Zeena?*" I half shout.
"It's getting loud in there! Let us in!" Sam's voice
calls while someone knocks three times—three
times again in short succession—Henri. Rhett opens
our door—Calvin's here, too, holding a mysterious,
tall skinny paper bag. Sam's got plastic cups; Henri,
a bag of ice. Alcohol's against the rules, but I don't
put up a fight. It's time these friends knew everything—
not just about Tim's call, but all about my family,
my search. I nod to Rhett. She says, "How nice
of you to bring refreshments! All right. Take a seat.
I have the feeling it's going to be a *very* long night."

Journal Entry #2195

Tim texted three times last night when we were all sitting on Rhett's side of the room, drinking rum and Coke. (Diet Coke for us girls.)

1) u ok? xo
2) Can I call?
3) Will call tomorrow. Promise xo

Finally, after much coaching from C&S, R&H, I texted him back:

"Ok. I'm glad." But no x's, no o's.

This morning, groggy with a drum beating steadily inside my head, I texted him again:

"Hi. Talk tomorrow. Too much going on today."

He called anyway, but I didn't answer.

He left a message: "Liz, please don't forget that I'm your friend forever. I'm here. I know you're going through a—stressful time. I'm *here*, really. . . . Okay, I'll try calling again. Tomorrow, like you said."

Lost

Like a balloon that's lost its string,
a feather that's lost its bird;
like a kingdom that's lost its king,
a poem that's lost its words;
like a dog who's lost his bark,
a library that's lost its books;
like a theater that's lost its dark,
a queen who's lost her looks—
that's how I feel, losing Tim.
Have to learn to live without him.

Journal Entry #2196: Calling Kin Solvers

First, Rhett and I have a gimlet at The Rock so I can calm my nerves. "Never mind Tim," she says. "You have so many people supporting you!"

Back at the dorm, she sits on my bed, watches me line up my artillery: Montblanc pen from Mom, pad of paper, cell phone. "Why not type notes into your laptop?" she wants to know. "I'm old-fashioned," I explain. "Born in the wrong century." "Me, too," she says.

Next to my laptop, Tim—the Hudson River just behind him—smiles at me from his photo, the one in the wood frame I bought at the Hello Shop. I make a move to turn him face-down, then change my mind.

My hand shakes as I dial the number. Rhett says, *"Breathe."*

Karen Mason picks up on the second ring. From Joe, I know that she's Kin Solver's founder, a birth mother. My words tumble out like toys from an overstuffed closet—a big, bright mess, from the look on Rhett's face. Karen, I think, is used to this. She doesn't interrupt.

When I finally give her a chance to start asking questions, I feel my heart start to beat more normally. Her voice is soothing, soft and silvery. She explains that she won't know if she can help until she has a chance to look over what I'll need to send her, but says she found her own birth daughter years ago, and then started applying all she'd learned in her own search to help others. "I've got a pretty good track record," she assures me.

Maybe I'm fooling myself; maybe I'm an incurable optimist—but when Karen and I hang up, I think, *She'll do it. She'll find her.*

Journal Entry #2197: The Deal

(From my notes talking with Karen Mason)

1) Send Karen everything I have so far—my non-identifying information that The Foundling sent last spring; what I'd just learned from Sophie. (Karen didn't seem phased by "Smith.") A copy of my birth mother's letter. (It seems too private. But I have to trust...) A list of any other details I can think of, like things Mom & Dad told me, even if they seem insignificant— how my b.m. named me Elizabeth Ann before my parents did, that my birth certificate is dated two years after I was born (send a copy).

2) Karen will review what I send & let me know within two weeks:
   a) if she can't help (no charge!)
   b) if she thinks she can help and how long it might take. If she can: cost ~$3,000 (!)

3) If (b), then I don't pay until Karen finds her, at which point Karen will contact me. I'll overnight the $$ (bank check/money order); when she gets it, she'll email me all of my b.m.'s info.

Rhett: That seems fair.

Kate: You know Mom wants you to be happy. Me, too! And it's not really that much money. Call her *now*.

Jan: I've got your back. Let me know if you need money.

Jade: I wish they had investigators like that in Korea . . . I'll light a candle for you, Liz.

How I long to call Tim! But Galileo has me thinking. We're talking about the Scientific Revolution in my Social Foundations class—that guy would rather spend the rest of his life under home arrest than give up his belief in Copernicus' theories. And that's got me thinking about <u>LOYALTY</u>. Where the hell is Tim's?

But I wish he weren't so far, not just physically but emotionally. I wish Cathy were here—she can't get home from Mexico soon enough.

But Rhett is here. And Kate. And Henri, Sam & Calvin . . . because OH MY GOD, this is going to happen. I'm going to find her—I just know it.

I Feel as if I'm Living a Fairy Tale

"Selkies are mythological creatures found in Scottish, Irish, and Faroese folklore . . . Selkies are said to live as seals in the sea but shed their skin to become human on land."—WIKIPEDIA

I'm a Celtic selkie
who's lost her skin,
hasn't been home
to her ocean since
then. And sometimes
I'm a mermaid
who gave up her fins
for the love of humans
who took her in. Now
there's a chance
I might crack open
all spells, spill back
into the sea that once
laid claim on me.

Journal Entry #2198

Email to Mom (easier than calling)
b.c.c.: Kate, Bob, Jan (included Tim, then erased him)

Hi Mom,

I hope you're well, and by now have forgiven Butter for chewing your favorite hat. You have to admit it's amazing that this is the *first* bad thing he's done! Well, except for opening the fridge and eating that steak . . .

So . . . Joe Alley gave me the name of a private investigator to help me with my search. I can explain how it works, but I don't pay anything unless they find something. Then it'll be $2,900. If you can lend me the money, I'll pay you back in installments—starting later this summer when I'm home and working at the Hello Shop again. Or I'll sell my car.

This is hard, I know . . . thanks for understanding, Mom.

> Love,
> Lizzie

Mom's response:
Lizzie, call me? This is all fine. Your father and I wanted this for you and now—I will give you the money.

See attached.

> Love,
> Mom

Attachment: Photo of Mom wearing a new purple knit hat. Butter also wearing a purple knit hat, complete with holes where his ears stick out.

Kate: She'll give you the money! Wow—this could really happen now, Lizzie! Call me!

Jan: I'll give you the money if your mom somehow can't. WOW, I had no idea you'd call them this fast! Talk soon?!

Bob: Ms. Smith, can lend you some $ but don't have whole $2.9K. LMK. Have to say I worry about you.

...I call Bob when I get that email. After he tortures me with the obligatory California weather report (always "sunny, 75"... too much like Florida's weather. Trying not to think of Florida), I ask him, "What's to worry about? You and Mom—you're both over-reacting."

"You don't know what—who—you're going to find, Lizzie," he says. "This person could not only reject you. *Again.*" (I cringe.) "It could be worse than that. She might be homeless. She could be a drug addict. She could be just waiting for a nice girl like you to come along and pay all her debts or pay her dealer or—"

"STOP, Bob," I insist. "I've thought this through, thought of every possibility. But I have to trust my instincts. I really believe in my soul that it's going to be fine—she wants to be found, and she's not...what you imagine."

We drop it after that. I almost tell him about the letter. If he read her words, he'd know I'm right.

Tim has tried calling twice, but I won't pick up. He didn't leave a message. I wish he had.

Journal Entry #2199

On my way to Social Foundations class, I mail everything off to Kin Solvers. It's like mailing off my soul. I say a little prayer, or try to—what to ask for? That they find her soon? That she welcomes me? That she's not a lunatic, or what Bob thinks? That she be *alive?*

After class I break down and call Tim. He's promised to be with me on this ship—and I need to hear his voice. The second I hear him—and how relieved he is to hear *my* voice—I think, maybe he *is* still loyal... as a friend. Then I sense I'm about to cry, so pretend I have to go before I really do. He does say one thing that keeps ringing in my head: "You're doing the right thing."

Now, I wait. Now, I just *have* to focus on my school work.

It's All in Kin Solvers' Hands Now

and it feels as if I've lit a fuse to a bomb
embedded in my heart—if I don't use
my head phones, if I don't keep busy,
I hear it tick, tick, tick ... any queasy
minute I could get a text saying, "Check
your email." Is it possible to fail
at waiting? Is it possible to refuse to
fret? Dad would calm me, urge, "No
regrets." He'd say, "Turn to poetry—
your muse will help defuse that bomb.
Meanwhile, it could take months
for that text to come. Meanwhile, live
this dream you're in, and what the heck—
allow yourself to have some fun!"

Rough

Today Ruth's wearing a tan bandana, the kind Kate wears
when she's cooking. Her hair is shorter than Jan's ever was—
as if she'd shaved her head and it's just growing back. "Look
who's here," she says as I approach. Someone's on my bench,
so she pats the space next to her. "Was starting to think you
disappeared," she says, unwinding a broken guitar string from
its metal peg with a pair of pliers. "Just living at the library,"
I answer. She glances at me, then gives each tuning peg
a twist, cuts the remaining strings. "Rhett says I've become

a hermit," I add as Ruth works, "but that's what I do when I'm—
when I need to focus." Ruth looks at me, those brown eyes so
attentive. "When my dad died last year," I add, "I spent a lot
of time in my room." Why did I say that? Because it's another
weight on my heart, another wire I'm trying to walk across
without falling off. Ruth lays her pliers between us on the bench.
I feel like that guitar—all that potential, but useless without its
strings. "Liz, I'm sorry," Ruth says. "You're too young to lose—
that had to be rough." I stare at her stringless guitar. Something

tells me Ruth knows about rough. "The anniversary is next
month," I tell her, "April first." Ruth picks up her pliers, points
them at me. "That's enough to make anyone want to hide
in the library," she says, pretending not to see the tears gliding
down my cheeks. Reaching into her guitar case, she pulls out
a new set of strings. *Oh,* I want to say, *my life is so much more
complicated than you can imagine.* "I've had some big losses
in my life, too," she offers. "And as soon as I get this thing
rockin' again, I'll play something happy just for you."

Rise On Up

"Although your soul
is full of woe, although
your heart is feeling
low, rise on up! Let it
all go," Ruth sings,
her husky voice so
different from Luka
Snuff's island richness,
but pitch-perfect just
the same. Until now
I hadn't noticed
how the sun is
shining on the arch,
how a bird I can't
name is twittering
in the tree behind
us. Shuffling by
with his mini-flock,
Pigeon Man waves.
The birds on his
shoulders, the bird
on his head seem to
bob with the music.
They all look so
carefree. Why not?
Why shouldn't I be?
Really, I'm the lucky
one. I'm sick of
stressing all the time.
Suddenly it seems
something inside me
is about to take flight.
"Rise up, rise on up!"
I sing along, "Your
cloudy old world
will soon be bright."

Journal Entry #2200

It's Ruth's left side I sit on, listening while a crowd gathers. When she plays I mostly focus on her fingers, long like mine, on those strings. Wishing I could play. Trying not to steal too many glances at her, though I do, here and there. I sit up straight, as she does. Funny I always seem to see her sitting down, but up close I can tell she's tall. I think we even wear the same shoe size.

Now she's playing "When You Never Said Goodbye" again. This song is about ME. I like singing along softly to the chorus:

> Wish I could climb inside
> myself, tumble down
>   tumble down
> to a past I never knew—
> maybe I'd reach the day
> when maybe you said *Be good*,
> when maybe you said *Don't cry*,
> when maybe you said
>   *I love you*—
> when you never said goodbye.

It isn't until the song ends—I'm clapping along with everyone else—that I see it. The little point on the edge of her left ear. Mine's on the right ear. Bob used to call me Spock Junior, sometimes Half Spock, when we were kids.

Poetry Walks

After workshop, Louise and I get huge cups
of tea at the Third Rail, then walk back up
and over to Goddard. This has become
a habit I've failed to mention to anyone,
especially Rhett—this time with Louise
something I look forward to, like a breeze
after a climb up a mountain. Mainly we
talk about people in class, and poetry—
Kamilah Aisha Moon, Richard Blanco,
Ruth Stone, Heather McHugh, Gary Soto.
Which poets we like best changes week
to week. With fiction, she likes it bleak:
Edward P. Jones and Cormac McCarthy,
Flannery O'Connor and J.M. Coetzee.
Me, I like my stories short: Grace Paley,
Louise Erdrich, Dan Chaon (an adoptee,
too). Today Louise says, "Hey, NYU's
lit magazine, *West Tenth,* comes out soon.
It's one of the best college journals. We
can apply for spots on its staff next week—
Would you want to try?" I choke on my
ginger tea. We laugh. "Oh, yeah! Would I!"

Journal Entry #2201

This afternoon we're all at The Rock when I make a comment about the bathroom there being "as dirty and dark as Pittsburgh." Calvin says, "¡Woah, *cállate, amiga!* What do you know about Pittsburgh?"

Nothing. I have to admit that I have never even been to Pittsburgh. But I've seen pictures of those old abandoned steel mills and remember some song about smoke and smog, about deserted streets and falling-down houses. Well, according to Calvin, Pittsburgh is a happening, college town with lots of cool music and stuff going on. But best (Calvin knows how to impress me) is that an amazing number of poets come from there: Terrance Hayes, Jan Beatty, Li-Young Lee, Jack Gilbert.

That's the last time I diss Pittsburgh, Calvin's home town. He writes fiction but reads a ton of poetry. Says poetry teaches him about compression and word choice. What did I do to deserve such cool friends?

Now I'm thinking, what if my b.m. lives in Pittsburgh? She could be anywhere. Why do I keep wanting to believe she's here—not even upstate, in her beloved "country," but in NYC, in *Manhattan?*

St. Patrick's Day Haiku

Green bagels, green beer,
green dog biscuits: even they
are Irish today

Frozen: My First Student Reading/ Mixer at the Café Du Monde

Like a snow woman. Like a deer in the road
at midnight. Like the lions on the library steps.
Like the statues of saints in church—only
my face isn't serene. It's a gargoyle face,

it's that deer's face; it's wide-eyed terrified.
I'd thought I could read a poem before a crowd
but instead I'm stuck in my seat, unable to
stand. Louise read her "Loud as Silence" poem

and then some guy Pete read "How Lance
Romance Got His Groove On," and now
it's my turn. My cheeks burn, my heart sputters
but my feet won't move. The MC sees me

seize, artfully calls the next reader. I think,
Some poet you are, Lizzie McLane. Rhett
leans toward me from her seat, whispers,
"It's okay! No blame! No beating yourself up!"

Calvin leans in, too: "Next time, you'll just have
a drink first. We'll sneak in a thermos of my
magic potion. That will set you in motion!"
Sam and Henri nod like the bobble-heads

on the dash of Bob's car. Calvin won't let me
make sour grapes out of this. "You'll read like
you're famous, a poet at the peak of her powers."
It's a sweet promise, but what I need is practice.

Journal Entry #2202:
A Few Days Before Spring Break

When we were all leaving the café last night, Louise caught my arm and said not to worry; she'd had all fall to practice reading for a crowd, and only now was she starting to feel comfortable in front of that microphone. Rhett gave me a weird look, like, "What the freak—?", but I thanked Louise with a gush of relief, realizing then I hadn't really been *breathing.*

Oh, but I still felt like a loser. Later, it turned out Calvin was right—after two of his rum & Diet Cokes, I was ready to read to everyone in Washington Square Park. But of course that was after dark, and beyond the five of us, hardly anybody was there.

––––––

Later, same night: Mom calls to tell me she's already started cooking—veggie lasagna, pea soup, three-bean chili, banana bread—to celebrate my coming home for break. She even stocked up on soy milk for my coffee. "I wish I could teach Butter to stir a pot or chop a carrot, but he's very good at keeping the kitchen floor clean," she says. "Of food, that is. His hair and muddy footprints are another thing."

Also have a date with Jan & Jade at Gertie's Diner, our old hang out. (Mine & Tim's too . . .) Jan says New Hook will seem boring after New York, but I told her no way. She also thinks that Bob is just projecting his own fears on my search—but she still reminded me that, instincts aside, I need to be prepared for *anything.*

––––––

Minute ago, text from Tim: "Wish I were going home next week. U know I have a tournament. Would rather see U. Talk soon?"

I write back, "Good luck. You'll be great."

I'm his friend, but obviously this Zeena is, too—I'm confused. And "When You Never Said Goodbye" continues to play in a never-ending loop inside my head:

Once I met the great wizard
of heart-ache—his mask was the sea—
I pled for his pity.
The wind blurs
then snuffs the star lights out.
There are just some things
it can't live without.

. . . and with that, I think it's time to switch off my lamp, get some sleep.

Holy Buttered Popcorn!

"Buttered popcorn and Coca-Cola:
another fine dining experience
brought to you by Calvin Casanova."
Calvin makes a bow. "You never
mince on quality when it comes to
snacks," Henri says, holding up
her cup to toast him. We're sitting
in the third-floor hall. Cheery music
wafts toward us from a ukulele
played by a girl I've seen but don't
know. "Ruth plays this song," I say.
"That's right," says Sam, snapping
his fingers. "Dan used to go see her—
meant to mention that, Liz." Calvin
groans. "Dan's my man, but we part
ways when it comes to musical taste,"
he says. Rhett nods, adds, "Hey, Dan
will go with you if she plays the clubs
again!" "*No, I'll* go with you," says
Sam, doing a little sit-dance. "Ignore
my roommate. Who besides Calvin
and Rhett doesn't like Ruth Smith?"

Journal Entry #2203: *RUTH SMITH?*

I just about spit my Diet Coke when Sam says Ruth's last name. Good thing I'm already sitting on the floor. Rhett's head whips around so fast I hear it crack like a knuckle. All I can say is, Holy Crap.

Rhett puts her hand on mine. "There are *millions* of Smiths, Liz. That's part of the problem, right? Don't read into this—"

"I'm not," I say, but we both know I'm lying. I can see Sam's eyes grow wide as it dawns on him—Henri and Calvin realize what we're implying at about the same time.

"Shit," Sam says. He looks stunned. "I never put that together."

"But as Rhett says, there's millions of Smiths—in New York alone!" Henri adds.

"What are the chances?" Calvin asks. We all stare at him.

"RIGHT," says Rhett at last. "Things like that only happen in the movies. Or in a Charles Dickens novel."

Surprise in Profile: Washington Square Park

Just as I'm closing my book, *Oscar Wao,*
the day so mild I don't need mittens now—
I get an odd sense someone's watching me.
Ruth's not there. I gaze around, pretending
to stretch—I look left, and that's when I see

Sam, sketchbook on his lap, putting away
his pencils. "Are you drawing me?" I say.
He sort of peeks over, cheeks sunset pink.
"Not now," he says, his smile so loony I
wonder for a second if he's had a drink.

Smiling back, I say, "I hate my profile."
He leaps up from his bench. "Oh, Liz! I'll
show you how beautiful you are!" Before
I can stand up, he's sitting beside me,
saying, "If I'd only had a few more

minutes, I'd have finished. Can I show you?"
His sketchbook is already open. I do
want to see, but my head's also spinning
like the break dancers by the fountain—
the image blurs. Why is Sam sketching

me? What Rhett would give to be in my place!
Doesn't he get—but wait, is that my face
in profile? "You don't know, Liz—that's one
reason I like you so much," Sam says. "Know
what?" I ask, staring down at what he's done,

what a miracle he's made with a pencil.
I actually look—well, pretty. "Sit still
for five minutes?" He digs in his backpack,
pulls out another charcoal pencil. Tim
used to photograph me gazing up at trees, back

when—"Sam," I say, "this is crazy." He looks
so sad. I sigh, "Five minutes," pick up my book.
He jumps up again, runs back to his bench.
Don't ask me out, I think. Imagining
how hurt Rhett would be gives my heart a wrench.

A Flattering Complication

"You could be a model," Sam says as we stroll through the park toward Goddard Hall. He's got a way with words—he sweet-talked that second-floor R.A. after our baby powder escapade—but this is over the top, the silliest thing I ever heard. Smiling my thanks, I change the subject to spring break. "You going to Florida with your brother?" Another boy would have taken the bait, but not Sam. He laughs. "Okay, I won't say how pretty you are for the rest of the day." (We stop to let an old man pass; I don't say a word.) "And yes, I'm heading to the beach with Dan, because he has all the money." Now I laugh, too. Sam opens the front door to Goddard, greets both security guards as we pass through the turn-stiles. "So, Liz," he says as we wait for the elevator, which is going down. "Where are *you* heading, and am I allowed to say that I'll miss you?" Rhett can't know any of this.

Journal Entry #2204

Rhett's packing, so our room looks as if it was toppled by a surprise tornado—sweatshirts, jeans, bras, shoes, empty water bottles everywhere.

She makes a joke about moving my poetry books. At least she's open about liking Sam now, but geez, what timing! I can barely look her in the eye for fear I'll blurt out everything that just happened with him.

That Sam is *smooth,* him and his pencil smell. Bob always said I'm too naïve—am I, really?

How can I feel guilty? Rhett just can't know. By the time we get back from break, this all will have blown over.

Henri, wearing her dragon slippers, just popped her head in to say goodbye—she's soon off to Boston. She says she wishes she were going to North Carolina like Rhett. Rhett says she'd go to Boston in a heartbeat. And did we hear Calvin's going to Boston, too, to see an uncle who teaches at Harvard, Henri wants to know? Rhett looks odd. Jealous, almost. She shrugs, tosses *Bleak House* into her suitcase. It seems she does know that.

Me, I'm glad to be heading to New Hook, though pray Kin Solvers doesn't text me while I'm there. I'm totally not prepared for anything to happen when I'm *home.*

Tim sends a text: "Hi to ur Mom tomorrow. & Butter."

He might be the only one who hears about Sam Paris. I text back, "I will," and send it with a kiss. Maybe Zeena will happen to see it.

Holy shit. I hope he's not sleeping with her.

. . . I just think of that NOW?

Home on Break / Break for Home

For most of the train ride home
I stare out my window at the river—
watch a rusty blue tug boat take its time
lugging an oil barge north; follow
a little iceberg with my eyes until
it's floated too far south to see.

At the Poughkeepsie station, I see
Mom and Butter ready to take me home,
red bandanas around their necks. Until
this moment, I would have bet a river
of dollars Mom would never wear red, or follow
a dog wearing red, with a red leash. Time

changes people, I know—but the one time
I bought her a red scarf, she said kindly, "See,
Lizzie, it clashes with my hair." I follow
them out of the station after much hugging. Home
is forty minutes north; less if we could take the river
instead of a road. Mom talks about Butter until

we pull in the driveway. It's not until
we're in the kitchen that she asks, "How much time
might it take Kin Solvers to find"—and a river
of words runs through my mind. Can she see
words puffing from my ears like smoke? *The home
fires are burning,* I think, then realize I didn't follow

all she just said. "Sorry, Mom—I didn't follow
you," I say. We talk over a pot of tea until
Kate calls, wanting to know if I made it home
okay. Then Butter jumps up from his bed: time
for his walk. Besides his kitchen bed, I see
one in the living room, one in Mom's studio, a river

of beds, it turns out, wends around the house, a river
of bones, balls, stuffed cows and monkeys follow
this river end-to-end. Bob's room, I see,
has been turned into Butter's room—that is, until
Bob comes to visit (that won't be 'til Christmas time).
My room, so far, is Butter-free, feels most like home.

In bed I dream I'm swimming in the river; until
I see Mom on shore, I feel lost. She shouts it's time
to follow her, waves that it's time to come home.

At Gertie's Diner

Waiting for our food, I tell Jan and Jade
how my mom's lost her mind over Butter.
They're not sure which is funnier: that
the cookie jar now is loaded with dog
biscuits, or that Bob's baby blanket covers

the royal, three-sided, therma-rest dog
bed in Mom's room. It feels good to laugh,
be with these friends. Jan looks happier than
I've seen her. Ever. "Hey, not to put an end
to the jocularity," she says after our waitress

sets down our omelets. "What's up with
Kin Solvers?" Really, this was why I needed
to see them so fast—I couldn't wait two more
days, when we'd said we'd meet—Karen
Mason had called to say YES, based on what

I'd sent, they believe they can locate my birth
mother in three to six months. Jade gasps,
leans into Jan, who says, "That's not long
at all, Lizzie. It takes some people *years!*"
I nod, take a deep breath, then a bite of toast.

"How can you think of anything else?" says
Jade. "I'd have to take a break from school!
I'd be a mess, thinking any day I might get
that text!" Jan nods, chewing thoughtfully.
"Such mental and heartfelt torment," I think—

my birth mother's letter reveals an anguish
deeper than this. "School's a good distraction,
even if it's hard to focus," I say. Jan's decided
not to go to college since she's taken over
Mack's Auto from her dad. But she understands.

"And don't forget," she says, "Liz has poetry
to keep her sane." But now I don't want to talk
about poems or school or Karen Mason or
the search or Rhett or Sam or even Tim.
The truth is, I want to talk about Ruth.

Journal Entry #2205

Karen Mason called again—thank God both times she's called, Mom has been out walking Butter.

My conversations with Karen aren't a big secret, but talking about my search with Mom is worse than having to talk about sex. We'd both rather talk about Butter, who has actually learned how to fetch Mom's slippers. Next, he'll be driving the car.

Back to Karen: she's given me a list of things to ask Sophie. I could ask them over the phone, she says, but it's best to go back to The Foundling in person—"You tend to find out more that way." That's for sure.

The list:

1) Confirm maternal grandparents were born in Scotland.
2) Was grandmother a nurse, or nurse's aid? (degree = the question)
3) Did grandparents continue careers as baker/nurse here in the U.S.?
4) Does b.m. live in tri-state area? (Sophie might not be able to answer this, but push for as specific information as possible.)
5) Name of doctor who presided over my birth? (Unlikely Sophie can reveal this, either, but try.)

I have this recurring feeling that I'm living a movie, starring me. But where's my script? What happens next, and next after that?

———

Text from Rhett: OMG you MUST read *Bleak House.* Esther = adopted ... birth mother just revealed! Wont give it away. (Hope alls ok there.) xoxo

The Butter Cure

Mom should know it will stun me.
She says, "Come in" when I knock
on her bedroom door. I enter—

and there is Butter, stretched out
on Dad's side of the bed like a sun-
bather on the beach. Mom looks

serene, propped up on pillows, a book
in her hands. The air smells faintly
of lotion—mandarin orange—and of

dog. Mom always said that if Dad
weren't allergic, we'd have a dog—
but it would never be allowed

on the furniture (as they are at Aunt
Marge's house), much less our beds.
"Mom," I say, "Butter sleeps *here?*

On your *bed?*" "Yes," she replies
matter-of-factly, "unless he kicks
me out. Then I sleep on the couch."

My chin must be near my knees,
it's dropped so far. "Mom, you sleep—
Butter kicks you out?!" A laugh,

soft as Butter's fur, escapes her.
"Lizzie, I'm kidding," she says,
laying her book aside. She pats

the bed for me to come sit. Butter
wags his tail; its thumps are muted
on the mattress. Reaching over

with one hand, Mom rubs his ear.
"Butter has given me a much-needed
gift," she says, putting her free hand

on mine. "I've been—" she stops.
Her face looks fragile, as if it might
break. But a faint smile radiates

underneath all that sadness, as
an unseen sun brightens a cloud.
"All of my excitement over Butter

probably seems—well, a bit
outrageous." Suddenly I want
to protest—No, no it doesn't.

Mom takes a deep breath, starts
again, "But a dog's joy—it's so
simple. And very, very contagious."

Journal Entry #2206

I've been blind as a newborn mouse. Blinded by my own stuff. Poor Mom! She's been so lonely! And, duh, she misses Dad maybe even more than I do.

When Mom and Butter come back from their walks, he greets me as if we've been parted for years. It's true—it's impossible not to smile when Butter's around. Mom is almost like her old self again. Almost. She'll never be the same person she was when Dad was alive—but neither will I. Neither will Kate, or Bob. We're just—different. But that's okay. That's what happens when someone you love dies. Like stars, the dead keep on shining, making bright new constellations in the galaxy of your heart.

I want to bury my face in Butter's fur and thank him. I think Dad's ghost already has.

Three Mothers

It was here on this bench beside the river
in New Hook that I used to sit during
my lunch break and think. It was here
I wrote a poem about a party where I had
too much to drink. Here that Tim first
kissed me, his arms a shield from all I
feared. How I could use those arms now,
knowing any minute, any day news of my
birth mother will turn my life upside-
down. It can't be otherwise, I realize—
even if she's my dream mother, best-
selling author who's been drowning
in sadness, trying not to remember
the day she surrendered me to social
workers at The Foundling. As if
the universe is reading my mind,
a woman strolls by with a baby
strapped to her chest. "Mama's best
little girl," the woman sings softly,
words that soothe and sting me.
She stops to gaze at the river, molten
glass flowing south toward the city.
The baby can't be more than a couple
of months old. At that age, a stranger
held me—not my birth mother, not
Mom, but another woman paid to be
my caretaker. A third mother of sorts—
I have to believe she was good to me;
I've always felt so loved. How would
this woman feel if she had to give her
child away? How could my first mother
do it, unwrap her arms, deliver me to
another, say farewell forever? *Such
heartfelt torment*—those words from
her letter keep whirling in my mind.
She felt so much sorrow. So why not

at least ask for an open adoption, where
we could be in touch? Was that too
much to bear? Wouldn't that be less
hellish than *this?* Perhaps someday
she'll tell me. Perhaps I'll never know.

Not Here

My father's disappearing from this house.
His navy wool coat's no longer hanging
in the closet; dress shoes, work boots, not
on the mud room floor. His robe doesn't
dangle from the back of the bathroom door,
eyeglasses don't rest atop today's *New Hook
Star.* His photo's in the living room next
to the couch, on Mom's dresser and taped
to the fridge, but his voice no longer rings
from the kitchen as he cooks, his hands
no longer bring in logs for the fire, slippers
don't wait beside his chair. His stack of books
lean now on a shelf, unread. *Dad, where
are you?* I call one night in a dream. *Dad,
I miss you,* I whisper to the morning sun.

Scrabble

My old friend Cornelius calls from out of the blue—
a bunch of friends from high school are going to
Noah's Ark to hang out and shoot pool about
eight o'clock tonight. "You have to come, Lizzie,"
he says. But they'll have to have fun without

me—I want to stay home and play Scrabble
with Mom, who made a yummy vegetable
stew for dinner and is now about to
open a bottle of wine. "Liz, are you sure
you don't want to go out? Your friends miss you.

You still have time," she says, but I assure
her I'm where I want to be. Butter
is stretched before the fire—"Watch out
you don't melt," I warn him. He thumps his tail
once, his eyes all dozy. There's no doubt

this dog knows he's landed in heaven. Mom sets
the Scrabble board on the coffee table, gets
two wine glasses from the china cabinet.
"You're not driving," she says, "you can have some
wine." "Butter, do you know where my Mom went?"

I ask this so seriously, Butter opens an eye, rises,
pads over to lick my face. I'm surprised
he doesn't join us on the couch, expecting
to play. Mom counts out our letter tiles—
"He'd cheat, anyway," she says, laughing.

Over cabernet, firelight, and words like "napkin"
and "poignant" I start to tell her all about Tim
and Sam, Rhett, Calvin, Henri, and Louise—
so many stories, we laugh hard when I spell
"restraint." "Well, Liz," Mom says, "I'm relieved—

don't take this wrong—I adore Tim, and think
he's right, though his timing *is* bad." Butter blinks
his assent. "You *should* date other people—
now's the time—and if you're meant to be— "
(she stops, her hand hovering with a tile

that turns out to be a "y," turning "leather"
into "leathery") "...you'll get back together."
"That doesn't mean—" (I use her "y" to write
"yonder")—"I should date Sam." "No. It means,
as your dad used to say, and he was right—

the universe is unfolding as it should." I want
to believe that, and wish it could apply to my
search and wherever that leads. Mom's thinking
the same. "Yes," she says, "that includes your
birth mother." We set down our glasses and hug.

Back at Mack's Auto

"Look, this Ruth *can't* be your birth mother. That's too crazy—
just because her last name is Smith, she plays songs for you
on her guitar, likes poetry—" Jan steps back from the hood
of a black car, shaking her hot-pink head. Suddenly my mouth
tastes like dread. "Don't even fantasize, much less hope—" she
stops when she sees my face. Perched atop my old metal stool,

breathing in the smell of gasoline and oil, admiring the tools
strung along the shop's walls, I'd felt content until the subject
of Ruth popped up again. Obviously, Jan's been pondering what
I told her and Jade at Gertie's the other day. "I know, I know,"
I say, "Ruth's even the right age, I think, but—damn. She can't
be *her.*" Jan wipes her hands on a rag, studying me. She's too

perceptive, knows me too well. The pink spikes of her hair are
dotted with the grease she's trying to clean from her forearms
and hands. Those hands. Capable as any man's. Now one is on
my shoulder. "Liz, you'll hear from Kin Solvers—maybe soon.
Then—well, I hope your story's happier than mine. But meanwhile, please don't write Ruth into some fairy tale you tell

yourself." Abandoned by not one mother, but two, Jan's no
believer in Disney-like stories. Hers could have been written by
the Brother's Grimm. I wonder if she's *too* cautious. But no.
She's just being realistic. She knows what's at stake. I try to
smile. "Coffee? Diet Coke?" she offers, glancing at the clock,
"Jade will be here in a while, and we both really need a break."

Journal Entry #2207

How fast do four greeting cards burn? In 1.3 minutes if you count the last paper embers brightening, then dying out like silent, miniature fireworks.

When Jade got to Mack's Auto after her class, we made a little ceremony out of incinerating the Christmas and birthday cards Jan's mom and birth mother mailed her. Of course, this was Jan's idea. She sometimes talks on the phone with her mom, who actually married that slick lawyer dude she left Mr. Mack for, but they moved to New Jersey and Jan doesn't see her. I don't know if that's Jan's choice or her mom's, but I fear it's the latter and so don't ask. As for "The B.M.," as Jan calls her—well, she sends two cards a year. So much for open adoptions. Some of them, anyway.

We burned the cards in a little black cast-iron woodstove Mr. Mack used to fire up when he needed to heat the shop. Now that Jan's taken over, she just turns on the thermostat, and the stove sits cold in its corner. As we stood there watching the flames, I thought how all three of us are puzzles with pieces missing, moons separated from our planets.

Jan says all of her anger and disappointment rises with the smoke every time she has one of these ceremonies. Maybe I should create something similar, a ritual to ease my nerves before I go back to The Foundling. The more I picture myself back in Sophie's office asking questions about myself and my blood relatives—questions I have every right to ask and have answered—I feel like someone who's been booed off stage, a poet smashed in the face by a rotten tomato thrown from the front row. Who threw it? My birth mother? "Lawmakers & the system"? History?. . . Me?

Visiting Dad's Bench:
Sacred Heart Cemetery

I stroke this marble
as if it is your face,
smooth after shaving.

Remember how, when
I was a little girl,
you'd chase me down

the hallway—your face
buried under a blizzard
of shaving cream—then

cover my cheeks with snow
kisses? I was your
captured snow girl. Your

mint-scented snowflake.
You'd carry me giggling
back to the bathroom,

hand down my blue plastic
razor with its cardboard
blade, and we'd peer into

mirrors (yours above
the sink, mine running
the full-length of the door)

and make our faces tingly
new. I didn't think you
could ever disappear,

leave me here alone to trace
the letters of your name
carved in stone.

End of Spring Break

"Next train to Grand Central Terminal will be leaving
from track two in eight minutes," booms a man's voice
over the loudspeaker as Mom pulls up to the Poughkeepsie
train station. In the back seat, Butter's panting. He knows
now what my suitcase means and probably feels the strain
of this goodbye. Mom and I aren't at each other's throats
as we were back in January—this is a tension we share.
A question mark dangles in the air above our heads like
a piñata about to crack. What secrets will it spill? Maybe
next time I see her I'll know my birth mother's first
name, maybe I'll know more than that. Where we'll go
from there, who can guess. Joe will give me tips. All I can
tell her now, I do: "Mom, I love you. You're the best mother
anyone could ever ask for." A March wind whips my hair
into my face as I step from the car. Caught in an updraft,
a plastic bag swirls past my head, then sinks. "Be a good
boy," I tell Butter. Then, *Brace yourself, Girl,* I think.

Journal Entry #2208

<u>Scene:</u> **Heading back to NYU on the train after Spring Break**

Out the window to my right, the Hudson River seems to flow in two directions. Like me.

So what did you do on spring break? asks an imaginary friend. *Oh, I moped, cried, hid from most friends, hung out with my Mom, visited Dad at the cemetery,* I answer. *You know, the usual things college kids do on break.*

It seems right to be on this train, heading south. My birth mother didn't want me to grow up in the city—well, I didn't, and I love the country, this wide river. But obviously my living in New York is meant to be. (So where, first mother, are *you?*)

―――――

The closer we get to Grand Central, the more my heart pounds like a prisoner in my chest. I close my eyes, sing "When You Never Said Goodbye" in my head. Two seats in front of me, a couple shares a bag of popcorn. The smell makes me nostalgic for Calvin's "cooking." I don't know yet how I'll deal with Sam—maybe just tell him I can't date someone who's so tan he makes me look as white as Florida's beach sand. (That won't work; he's seen Tim's photo.) Maybe I'll tell him I just need a while for my feelings about Tim to settle. Tell him meanwhile, Rhett—oh, forget it. She'd kill me.

―――――

A little while ago, a woman got on at Croton-Harmon, sat in the seat across the aisle from me. Her hair falls in loose, sparrow-brown curls around her shoulders. It's hard to tell, but she could be late-30s. My birth mother is 37, if The Foundling info was right. Cathy said there were mistakes in hers, stuff her crazy b.m. told her adoption agency. ("The Home for Little Wanderers." As if the babies there just wandered in off the street, asked if there were any parents around they could spare.)

There's a plastic scrish-scrish sound; the woman's eating potato chips. She catches me staring. Her eyes are dark. Brown. Her long gray coat, black cashmere scarf, designer-looking jeans, tall black leather boots practically reek of money. She could be . . . what number reunion fantasy is this? Maybe it will be better if my b.m. isn't rich. I don't want her thinking I want a relationship just because of that. Does my b.m. have kids? They'll like me better if they aren't worried about my taking a cut from their inheritance.

———

Entering the tunnel at Grand Central, text from Tim: "Hey, L. Hope u had great time in N. Hook. Talk soon? xo"

I answer: "Just back in NYC. Need some time. Hope you're ok."

———

Evening, text from Bob: "Mom painting Butters portrait. Sounds strangely HAPPY. Must be ur doing, or did u send ur angelic twin home 4 break?"

Kate & I Face Down a Demon on a Not-So-Cold Day in East River Park

To our right lies brownish lawn and picnic
tables where families celebrate birthdays
with yellow cake and butterscotch balloons—
where a juggler tosses china plates, where
a man with a sirloin-steak face brushes his
bulldog, where a hot Latina in a cornflower
sweater hula-hoops beside her daughters, all
bright as new coins. To our left, runners
lean and lank zip along a concrete path, near
the iron rail that marks the park's edge
and the East River's bank. Sunlight glistens
on the water, lends the scene a movie-set
feel. Across the river, Queens looks gray,
more cement than steel. Soon it's Brooklyn
we see—both boroughs part of the island
they call "Long." But as we stroll, it's clear
something's wrong. Kate's pulled up her
hood—I barely see the tip of her nose.
Silence has shoved itself between us like
a stranger who doesn't belong. It grows
louder as we walk. "Kate, *talk* to me,"
I finally say. Inside her jacket, my sister
seems to shrink. "Are you mad at me?"
I ask. The hood shakes, *No.* "So, what
is it? I don't know what to think!" I cry.
We stop. Kate spins, her face panicky
pale, then grabs me as if she's drowning.
"Oh, Lizzie, Lizzie," she whisper-sobs,
"What if you have another sister!"

Journal Entry #2209:
Sisterhood & Friendships

Early afternoon, we're drinking strong coffee, sitting on the 3rd floor outside Sam & Calvin's room, the one with the autographed Mind of Snow poster on the door. Stretched out in their sweats, the boys look like basketball players—their legs go on for miles.

My legs are sore from the long, long walk Kate and I took yesterday along East River Park, our silence broken by tears and finally honest talk. How could my love for Kate change because I find another sibling, sister *or* brother? With each step in this search, I only feel our sisterhood grow stronger. And as far away as he is, I suddenly feel closer to Bob, too. Protective of them both. Maybe that's how they feel about me, too. No one, not even a blood relative, is going to come between us.

By the time we got back to Kate's apartment, we were laughing, mostly over Butter stories. She says he stole Mom's paint brushes and buried them in the back yard. In the same hole, Mom found the TV's remote. Seems this was his revenge when she was spending too much time at her easel, or she was too busy watching *anything* but "Animal Planet." He'd watch "Animal Planet" for hours if that were possible. (When Butter sees a dog, he runs at the screen, then sits, barking.)

Henri's pulled her pony tail over her shoulder, begins to weave three strands into a braid. She's trying not to stare at Calvin, while Rhett stirs her coffee without drinking it. Meanwhile, Sam's telling us about this wild party his brother Dan threw ("Where were *we?*" Rhett wants to know.), while Calvin, half listening, scrolls through his iPod with a thoughtful look on his face.

Calvin came back from break with his hair in short cornrows. He almost looks like Cornelius Eady does on the back of *Autobiography of a Jukebox,* only his face is thinner. And Calvin wears glasses. Calvin has actually *read* Eady—discovered his poems when reading Terrance Hayes. Funny, I told him, it happened the other way around for me; reading Eady led me to Hayes. (*Flash:* Tim reciting Hayes's "Clarinet" in high school English class . . .) A while back, Calvin and I got talking about how the work of one poet can lead you to another. He found Hayes after reading Willie Perdomo. I found Mark Turcote by way of Louise Erdich. Poor Henri kept trying to join in by mentioning fiction writers who'd done the same for her. I hadn't heard of a single one except for David Capella, whose novel about a pyromaniac was just made into a movie.

Maybe I'll read Ruth a poem . . . I can just imagine her face . . . It seems we're all lost in dreamland this morning. Except Sam. Caffeine-jittery, he says something about the band at that party (all NYU students, I think), and then, *"Right* C?" He nudges Calvin with his elbow. Sleepily, Calvin says, "What's that?" Sam hesitates, then just says, "Drink some more java, my friend."

Rhett says, "A wild party with live music. That's what this little tribe needs!"

Peace Offering

Instead of holing up in the library with Aristotle
or hunkering down in my room with Wendell
Berry or *Ahora Hablemos Español,* I'm out
by the fountain in the park with Rhett, people-
watching. We take turns hatching stories:
the woman in the dark green raincoat is on
her way to meet her lover on West Tenth;
the couple walking their white poodle are
plain-clothes cops. That boy eating noodles
from a cardboard carton? Last night he wrote
a pop song that will soon make him famous.
Rhett's dreaming up lyrics when Louise walks
by—we're all surprised. She gives us a shy
wave and I say Hi, then turn to look at Rhett.
Who would have guessed it? Rhett hesitates,
then says, "Hey, Louise. Liz here has been
telling me that you're a really good poet."

In Workshop

(I bring in a poem I wrote during Winter Term, before I knew Ruth's name)

We critiqued "Ms. Guitar" in workshop today.
Few students are writing formal verse, so
this was a chance for Professor Aguero
to point out how form provides room to play—

most students write in free verse because they
think formal verse is too strict. They don't know
how form can stretch your limits, make you grow
as a poet in surprising ways.

Then she spoke about form and content, how
villanelles are perfect for obsessive
subjects. The form shows how the speaker in
the poem can't get "Guitar Woman" out
of her mind. "This doesn't need aggressive
work," she said, "only minor revision."

On Second Thought

Sometimes I'm like Bob,
trying to carry too many
grocery bags from the car
to the kitchen—so
of course one slips,

leaves a mess of eggs
and tomato sauce mixed
with glass and shells
in the driveway. That's
me: spring classes and this

"thing" called a search
already nearly too much
to carry, and now I'm
scheming with Louise
about how to become

an editor for *West 10th
Magazine.* Bob would
say, Put a cork in that
bottle; save it for later.
So I'm editing my plan.

This summer I'll take
NYU's program,
"Writers in New York,"
earn eight credits plus
four more weeks here

at Goddard after spring
term ends. I'll be living
my writer's dream for
real! Or, my life will be
truly insane by then.

Journal Entry #2210

New security guard in the lobby today. Of course, Sam introduced himself, shook her hand, asked her name while we were flashing our IDs, pushing through the turnstile toward the elevator. Digging through his pockets for his ID, he must have pulled out ten coupons (for Klong, Big B, the Third Rail). Reminded me of Mom at Kelly's Grocery Store. Rhett teased, "Life's too short to cut coupons!" Something, apparently, her mother used to say.

Sam's not acting crazy, as I worried he might when I got back from break. Maybe he realizes I'm not ready for another relationship—he knows how much I've got on my mind, as they all get an earful some nights when we sit up talking.

When he's tired, Sam rubs both eyes with the palms of his hands, and his eyeballs make this gross squishy sound. Last night Calvin said, 'Stop that, man—you sound like a B-horror movie."

A horror movie. That's what my stomach feels like lately. I'll be glad to get this next step with The Foundling *done.*

Determined: At The Rock

Clunk clunk clunk
                          clunk clunk:
the sound of five shot glasses
hitting the bar after we've each
slammed a Pineapple Bomber.
"Do not tell me what's in that
thing," Calvin instructs Clive,
the bartender; "It's too smooth,
too sweet—it's gotta be evil!"
My jaw, my shoulders, do start
to relax as I feel the liquor seep
through my stomach. We never
slam shots, but in light of the fact
that tomorrow I'm going back
to The Foundling, Rhett suggested
The Rock. Then Sam suggested
the shots. I guess I've been wired
since coming back from break.
When I called Sophie to make this
appointment, she sounded pleased
to hear my voice. That didn't cool
the fire I've felt smouldering inside
me since that day of Jan's card-
burning ceremony. "You okay?"
Henri asks. "You seem—" Rhett
says. She and Henri exchange
a knowing look, while the boys
pretend to study the bottles
behind the bar. "WHAT?"
I want to know. "Five more,"
Sam says to Clive, and I've got
that feeling I should say No,
but don't. Won't. "Like a bull
about to enter the ring," says
Calvin. "And the world,"
Rhett adds, "is wearing red."

Second Visit to The New York Foundling, Karen Mason's Questions in Hand

I'm no longer nervous. Now I'm pissed.
Not at Sophie, but the system she works for.
Why is it a crime to want to know who you are?

There is that folder—my life in Sophie's hands.
The story of my birth held tight, like a fist.
I'm no longer nervous. Now I'm pissed.

Were my grandparents born in Scotland?
Once here, was my grandma a nurse, grandpa a baker?
Why is it a crime to want to know who you are?

Was I such a danger? A big secret to protect?
My birth mother must have agreed to this.
I'm no longer nervous. Now I'm pissed.

Who was the doctor who delivered me? No one
will say. And my birth mother, does she live very far?
Why is it a crime to want to know who you are?

"I'm sorry," Sophie says, "No one deserves this.
I want to help, but can only go so far."
I'm no longer nervous. Now I'm pissed.
Why is it a crime to want to know who you are?

Journal Entry #2211

<u>Scene:</u> Sophie Fedorowicz's office

"WHY IS IT A CRIME TO WANT TO KNOW WHO YOU ARE?" I say too loudly. Then I just stare at Sophie. A strand of her short, gray hair hangs just above her left eye. Last visit, I had wished that—when I was her age—my hair would turn such a beautiful gray, like Professor Aguero's hair. Now I've decided I'll color my hair until I turn eighty. Now it's all I can do to stay in my chair, not leap up and rip that folder from her hands. Okay, so now I know both of my birth mother's parents were born in Scotland. And though my grandmother worked as a nurse, it's not clear how my grandfather made a living once he landed here. He was a baker in Scotland. That's as much as she could say. The folder is keeping the rest of its secrets. For now.

"I understand why you might be angry, Liz," Sophie says gently. She pauses, looks at me with such . . . kindness. As a mother would.

Sophie takes a deep breath. Then she says, "I am a social worker because I love children. I feel a strong kinship—and care especially for the children we have placed. Like you. Like your brother and sister. I can't imagine how difficult this search is for you. For your family. Maybe only orphans and other adoptees can truly empathize at your level, feel what you feel—but I *do* care. And I agree—the laws are not fair." She stops, her eyes glistening.

Sophie looks down at that folder, then at me. "Liz, for whatever reason, your mother signed those papers for a closed adoption. But based on her history, her letter—you know nearly as much as I do now—I have to believe she dreams every day of being found."

It takes me a while to pull myself together. Then Sophie walks me through a maze of offices and cubicles, down the elevator, then across the lobby to the front door. "Call me any time you need to, Liz," she says, "Even if it's just to talk. And—God bless, dear."

(Other) Mother

Mother—

> I will find you.
> I'm getting closer. Now,
> any day.

Mother—

> How will we speak?
> What will you say to me
> when we are at last alone?

Mother—

> When we meet
> wear no perfume.
> I will know you
> by your scent.

Mother—

> What is our story?
> How could you end it?
> We were so young.

Mother—

> What will our life be
> when we have found we?

Postcard from Cathy

Liz!

So happy to hear your Mom's doing better.
Your Butter stories had me falling off my
chair. And now I'm on the edge of it, as
you are, waiting for NEWS from Kin Solvers.
. . . BIG surprise: Jan wrote me. I was
so jealous you all hung at Gertie's (wow,
I could go for a cheeseburger & fries),
but happy her dad's selling the house.
So she and Jade are getting an apartment!
Where? All she said was "near the shop."
Isn't it great? Jade's so good for Jan
(she seems genuinely happy for once),
and it's about time she stopped serving
as her dad's maid. Now let's hope he moves
somewhere walking distance to O'Toole's
and stops driving drunk. They should set
up a bed for him under the bar! Anyway,
miss you and can't wait till June, as hard
as it will be to say goodbye to "my" kids.
Lots of tears around here these days.

> Con un abrazo,
> *Cathy*

p.s. growing out my hair again!

The Eye of the Storm Doesn't Last Long

(After I call Karen Mason with the few facts I learned from Sophie)

If my life were a canoe, I'd say I've been rushing
down rapids for months, a year—then suddenly
calm water surrounded me. I knew it couldn't
last: Kin Solvers could text me any day; classes
kick my butt, make me stay in the library way past
dinner; and then there's this nutty situation of men.
I miss Tim as a newly deaf person might miss
music. And here is Sam, ready to tango—yet
he must know as well as I do how Rhett likes him,
how loyalty to her means I can't even give an "us"
a waltz. So he keeps things light, flirts with her
and Henri as much as me, and I like him more
for that. But through it all, I've known the date
was looming; heard the thunder booming from
afar. Soon it will be April first, the day my father
died. Water's churning around me again, white
caps whipping in little waves. Then I see her,
Ruth walking toward me, guitar case in hand,
her head a mess of curls.

Journal Entry #2212

<u>Scene:</u> **Washington Square Park**

Ruth's face is sunnier than the day, which is bright and warm for late March. "Gorgeous morning," I say, strolling at a fast pace toward her. "Gor-geous, just like ya-self," Ruth says in an overdone New York accent. She *is* as tall as I am. And way less pale than usual. Resisting the urge to run to her, I think, *Could you be? Did you ever—?* She says, "We'll never score our bench today! Do you care—do you have time to sit over there on the marble bench? I have a song for you." Nodding, beyond pleased, I follow her, asking in my head, *Is it you? Is it?* But I can't bring the words to my lips. *Stop it, Lizzie,* I think. *You nut job. She's not.*

On the long marble bench close to the arch, we're surrounded by running kids, mothers with arms stacked with jackets, even a few early daffodils and tulips. I feel as awkward as Sam looked that day when I caught him sketching me. "Can I take your picture?" I manage to ask. Ruth nods, smiles, runs one bony hand through her new walnut curls while I fumble with my phone. I stand, snap a few shots, then settle on the bench beside her, words tumbling in my head like water over rocks.

Ruth looks straight at me, puts her hand on my arm. "I'm clean. Cancer-free," she says. My hand rushes up to meet hers. "I've not told you about—my treatments, but now," she hesitates—"Well, you *are* my friend!"

Oh, kind, caring Ruth. *Thank you, God,* I think, then give her a hug. "I'm so, *so* happy," I say, breathing in her scent, wanting to touch those curls. They don't yet cover the little point on her left ear. As if reading my mind, she puts one hand in her hair, says, "All this time, I've been wanting to tell you I'm a curly-haired girl, too—but they say once it's gone, you never know how it might grow back. It could have been as straight as your friend's, the Asian girl." "Henri," I say, and Ruth nods, "As straight as Henri's. But you—I've always admired your hair, Liz. Maybe in a year mine will be as long!"

I want to shout: *Ruth! Did you ever give up. . . ?* But I hear myself say, "Your hair is very pretty, Ruth," while she unhooks the hinges of her guitar case. Glancing up, she says, "I'm going away for a few weeks." I must look shocked. She touches my arm again. "Not far—Florida. To see my folks. They've been worried."

Her parents! I'd thought about siblings, but not grandparents, really, beyond the nurse/baker question. My mouth hangs open. Do I say, "Of course," or "How are they?" I hope I do, but am having trouble tracking what I say inside my head and what I say out loud. Ruth adjusts the guitar on her lap, strums and tweaks it back in tune. She says, "This is for you. I know you have a tough day coming up, and I won't be here."

She plays a song she says is by Livingston Taylor: "My Father's Eyes." I'm starting to listen to song lyrics with a new kind of attention. Lyrics are like poems, but different. They seem to need the music to make us feel their true power—like a play needs to be acted, or at least an actor's voice, for its words to have their full impact. This song is a kind of love-tribute to Taylor's father, full of admiration and longing to be as good a man as his father is. The way Ruth sings it—I swallow hard. At the end, I dry my eyes while the crowd that's gathered around us claps, cries, "Encore! Encore!"

Journal Entry #2213

I sent Ruth's photo to everyone—well, not Cathy, not Mom or Tim, but to Kate, Bob, Jan, Jade, Rhett, Henri, Sam, Calvin—with the question, "Who does this look like?"

Rhett: She has curly hair?!

Jan: Jade & I definitely see what u mean, but CAREFUL.

Calvin: Ruth Smith?

Sam: Whats her name. Orphan Annie. Only brown hair.

Henri: U w hair short!

Kate: Call me, L. xoxo

Bob: More like a McLane than any of us. Cousin Lucy? Aunt Marge?

(Kate thinks I'm setting myself up only to be let down: "Please drop this idea!" I told her what Bob said, though, and we had to agree that he's weirdly right.)

————

This afternoon, unable to focus, I'm cleaning our room like a crazy person. When Rhett opens the door, I'm standing on top of my desk with a rag in my hand, singing the chorus to "When You Never Said Goodbye." Henri peeks from behind Rhett, says, *"Liz?"* No use explaining.

Rhett announces that Sam's brother Dan is throwing another party, and we're invited. "So, start thinking outfits, girls," she says." "When we go," adds Henri, "let's stick together, okay?"

My Almost Party (With Parts I Don't Remember Filled in by Henri and Sam)

It hit me as soon as we all walked in the door:
hot guys in black T-shirts, girls in short skirts
with sky-scraper-long legs, candy-colored
jello shots and a bathtub full of beer . . . clearly
this was a party to rival any back home. Here
was a party where a girl could find trouble. And
count all that was on *this* girl's mind—make that
double. Bigger than I'd thought, Dan's apartment
thrummed with the bass and drums of Silent
Crimes. "I could use a drink," Rhett bellowed
in my ear. "Don't lose me!" shouted Henri

as Calvin and Rhett disappeared. "Don't worry!"
I yelled, though I doubted she could hear. From
the thick of the crowd came a guy in high heels;
he gave us each a drink, then flew away like
a bird into a cloud. Soon Sam was at my side—
he'd gotten here early to help Dan set up.
"You have to meet my brother," he said, handing
me another cup just as Rhett and then Calvin re-
appeared, each with extra drinks in hand. Rhett's
were nearly gone. "We having fun yet?" she said,
then, "Oh! I love this song!" "Good," said Calvin,

"because I long to dance." He put out his hand
and she took it, then she sashayed away in her
black and white dress without a second look
at Sam. This *was* our chance to let loose, a night
for me to forget school work, my search, even
Ruth and April first. I put an arm around Henri,
gulped my vodka punch in seconds. Sam
handed me another. "Do you really think Ruth
might be your mother?" His question made me
down drink number two. Or was that three?
"Birth mother. But let's not talk about it now,"

I said. Henri slipped out from under my arm.
"Vow you two won't move until I'm back?"
she asked. I nodded. Sam did, too, saying,
"Upstairs bathroom won't have a line." "*Two*
floors? Holy crap, Sam," I remarked, "No
wonder four guys live here." Sam shook his
head. "Five." He stared straight into my eyes
but I looked away. Darting between couples,
Henri looked fine in her little green dress.
I'd hoped Calvin would notice until he danced
off with Rhett. Now I hoped *she'd* not do anything

she'd regret. "Another stress reliever, at your
service," sang the guy in high heels—he and his
glittery gold pants had a way of knowing when
to show. "Dreamy," he cooed, eyeing Sam as we
took punch from his tray; made a curtsey before
gliding away. "I'd better slow down," I said to no
one in particular. Sam said, "Let's get some water
when Henri comes back." "Hey, are you keeping
track of these?" I asked, handing him an empty cup.
Two black girls squeezed by, holding each other up.
"How come your lesbian friends never visit?"

asked Sam as we watched the girls go. "Who?"
I said. Maybe I'd heard him wrong. "You know,"
he answered, "Jan and Jade." I nearly spilled my
drink. "What makes you think they're lesbians?"
I said. (And why did I feel angry?) "They're good
friends. Plus Jade works at Jan's shop. That's all."
I took a giant swig, wondering, *Are they?* Sam said
he didn't mean anything by it. As I looked around
for Henri, the room began to sway. "Liz, are you
okay?" I heard him say as I sank slowly to the floor.
Through my vodka-punch haze I managed to slur,

"Just kind of *warm*." Next thing I knew I was outside—
Henri and Sam each held me by one arm. "Where we
going?" I think I asked. Henri said, "*You?* Back

to the dorm." Trying to stand straighter, I cried,
"But the party just started! And Henri you didn't
dance with Calvin yet!" "Uh, Liz," Sam sputtered.
"*Liz,*" Henri hissed, "*Don't.*" That sobered me a bit.
I'd never made Henri pissed. "I won't, I won't,
Henri," I cried. "I'm so sorry. Romance sucks.
Don't I know. Doesn't it, Sam?" He shrugged.
Needless to say, I never did meet his brother Dan.

Won't I Ever Learn?

Up 'til now, I've been so proud of
how I've held my liquor—
partying just

enough to feel a buzz but not
lose control. "You're under
a lot of stress,"

sweet Henri said last night as she
helped me into bed. "No
excuse," I think

I cried, at least inside my head.
My poor head, throbbing like
last night's music.

Last summer, I was hung-over
nearly every Sunday.
I can't—I won't

be that girl again. No matter
what happens. With that vow
my headache starts

to fade. Then: a knock at the door—
Henri, with a bottle
of Gatorade.

After Henri delivered the Gatorade and I mouthed a big *THANK YOU*, she slipped out again, quiet as a pencil skimming paper. From the other side of the wall between our desks croaked Rhett's groggy voice.

Rhett: Who was that?

Me: Dad would say, an Angel of Mercy. Henri.

Rhett (silence, then): You okay?

Me: Been worse. Feeling stupid.

Rhett: You were gone before I realized—but Sam said you'd be fine.

Me: Sam? Of course—he went back. What time did you get in? I was comatose.

Rhett (silence again): I guess . . . six.

Me (impressed): The party went *that* long! Dang. I missed it. I really screwed up.

Rhett: Not exactly. . . I don't know. It's fuzzy. Between those crazy drinks and—Dan's friend had some good weed, so . . .

Me: You smoked pot? (Am I a total drip? A virgin who's never even tried pot?)

Rhett: It made me want to dance all night!

Me: Wow—and you and Calvin danced until six?

(Silence.)

Me (my brain waking, working): You were—you and Calvin?

Rhett: Sam slept at Dan's, so—

Me (hesitant): Rhett, I thought you liked Sam? I mean, I'm glad for you and Calvin—!

Rhett: I know! (I can tell she's smiling now.) Here I've been trying to convince you what a catch Calvin is—I guess I convinced myself instead. (pause) Besides, Sam likes *you*. You must realize that.

Me (thinking, *Ignore that.* Thinking, *Poor Henri!):* You two looked fab on the dance floor.

Rhett: Isn't he *amazing?* I've never been with someone who dances like that! So you can imagine how he—kisses.

Me (sitting up now, I gulp some Gatorade): Mmmm ... lucky girl. He *is* amazing, on so many levels.

I glance at my phone—texts from Tim and Sam. *Sam*—it hits me, what he said about Jan and Jade ...

Rhett: Liz?

I collapse back on my pillow—a few feathers fly out like little ghost-birds. One of these days, my old down pillow could use some TLC with a needle and thread.

Me: Rhett, it's only 10:30.

Rhett (pause): Right. Good night!

Her mattress creaks; I hear the rustling of sheets. A brief silence. Then— well, if she's been drinking, Rhett snores. I now know what a snoring, teenage bear probably sounds like.

Assumptions

We McLanes are a motley crew—
all sizes and shapes—some eyes
brown, others blue. Truly, my sister
Kate is Rose Red, while my brother's
Elmer Fudd. Yet when introduced
to someone new, my family, it's
assumed, is related by blood.

Henri counts on her fingers, passed
algebra by the skin of her knees;
chemistry, she claims, only makes
her sneeze. But because she's half
Chinese (and her father's a professor
at MIT), people assume (she laughs)
she excels at science and math.

Calvin can dance, but says he sucks
at basketball: *"All* black guys can't
play!" And though his last
name is "Paris," Sam can't speak
French at all. So just because Jan
and Jade are always together when
I call, just because they'd rather go
home than be with me on a Saturday,
just because they'll soon be roommates, do I assume they're gay?

Scratch "Are Jan and Jade gay?" You'd think I'd know, right? I mean, Jan and I have been friends since third grade. She would have shared something that intimate with me. I think that's why I was so mad when Sam suggested it—the idea that he would know that before I did, even if maybe it had crossed my mind in the past, seemed so wrong. But weirdly, they both called late last night to give me their new address, and to announce Jade's got a *boyfriend*. Funny, I'm actually disappointed. They'd make such a great couple! Will give Sam this news when I see him.

Jan said what a drag it was, moving in the rain and wind. It's poured sideways for two days. Coming around the northwest corner of Goddard Hall, I nearly blew backward into the man behind me. I tried to cheer myself: the rain will just make the flowers grow faster in the park.

Both yesterday and today I've seen Louise in the library. Had to tell her what I'd read— that the poet Alexander Pope was so blown away by Sir Isaac Newton's scientific accomplishments, he wrote this epitaph for Newton's gravestone:

> "Nature and nature's laws lay hid in night;
> God said 'Let Newton be' and all was light."

Louise said, "Isn't it cool when a class like Social Foundations kind of crosses over into a poetry class?" Mainly it got me thinking about what I could write for Dad's bench. Or my own gravestone.

Part of me wants to share my story, my search with Louise, but our friendship isn't quite "there" yet. I think I'm just wanting as many friends around me as possible when I hear from Kin Solvers. And when everybody leaves town at the end of the semester, Louise will still be here, uptown with her parents. But it's not like we're that close that I can share this with her . . . maybe at some point, if our friendship keeps growing. Still, I can't count Louise on the list of buddies who will be here for me when I need that. With every day that goes by, Karen Mason must get a little closer to finding something. Finding *her*.

April First

No one will play me for a fool. Not today.
Rhett's made sure of that. She and Henri left
a card taped to the bathroom mirror, hand-made
(Rhett drew the picture of both of them: their dark
hair is black thread; clothes, real fabric). "Through
thick & thin, we're here for you!" it read.

Kate I'd see later. Bob sent a text that read
"Bear hug. Love." "Thinking of u today,"
read Tim's. Before calling Mom, I had to get through
Spanish. I'd meant to look up "headache," but left
my dictionary back at the dorm. Senora Arroyo's dark
eyes blinked at *"Mi cabeza está mal,"* my made-

up way of saying, "Don't expect me to talk today." She made
a sympathetic face. *"Ah, usted tiene un dolor de cabeza."* I did read
a Neruda poem out loud, "Horses," set in a "dark
Berlin winter"—*Berlin oscuro.* It seemed that today
was perfect for miracles lighting up all that winter left
so otherwise bleak. So it was poetry that got me through

Spanish class. What could possibly get Mom through
this morning, this day? When I called, she'd just made
peanut butter dog biscuits. "He'd eat them all, if left
to his own devices," Mom said of Butter, though she read
online *some* dogs stop eating once they're full. "Today
he can have a few extra," she said. "Next comes dark

chocolate cake, but Butter can't have chocolate, dark
or milk. Makes dogs sick." So baking would get Mom through
the morning at least. I asked, "And the rest of today,
Mom? What will you do?" Her friend Isabel made
them a dinner reservation; otherwise, she'd read,
take Butter to the cemetery. I could see it: left

on Parker, right on LaGrange . . . Dad's bench is left
of the clump of pines. Mom knew this was a dark
day for me, too, but I assured her I had tons to read
and would see Kate; my friends would see me through
the rest of the day. Sure enough, when I made
it back to the dorm, a bouquet was waiting. "Today

going ok?" texted Tim—the yellow roses from him, who threw
his arm around my shoulder, who listened, who made
me feel all might *someday* be okay, a year ago today.

The Rest of April First

Almost like the "old days" (six weeks ago),
Tim and I spent an hour on the phone.
We laughed—Zeena, it seems, is known to throw

a tantrum if she doesn't get her way.
Otherwise, she's "very nice," and sometimes
lets him win a round of golf. "You could say

he's from Mars, Zeena's from Pluto," jokes Rhett.
"Pluto's not even a planet anymore," I say.
"Exactly." Hey, I don't expect to forget

my grief, but laughing sure does help. My friends
gave me that gift all evening—first Henri
showed up with a pizza, then Sam and Calvin

with a bottle of merlot and a toast:
"To Liz: you're the girl we admire most." *

* followed by assurances to Rhett and Henri that they admire them
 "most," too

Decision: Ruth

Why torture myself with being unsure?
We've so much in common—she *could* be my mother.
When Ruth gets back, I'm going to ask her.

Don't I already have enough pressure
searching for that "she," my other mother?
Why torture myself with being unsure?

We both love music, spending time in nature,
poetry, too—is it so odd that I wonder?
When Ruth gets back, I'm going to ask her.

Why not take all possible measures
in searching for the one I call "birth mother"?
Why torture myself with being unsure?

Kate fears I'm setting myself up for disaster.
But Ruth's last name *is* Smith! She might be my mother.
When Ruth gets back, I'm going to ask her.

Thank God—Ruth is beating her cancer.
Still—it could be now or never.
Why torture myself with being unsure?
When Ruth gets back, I'm going to *ask* her.

Do-Over at the Café Du Monde

I down a rum and Coke before we go,
so I'm not even shaking as we glide
into the room where the microphone
looms on its little stage. But my faux
confidence flies away like a scrap
of paper in the wind when Professor
Aguero strolls in. *Please, no.* Looking
around for Louise, who's sitting near
the back, I see she's as shocked as I am.
"Chill, Liz, you're ready to rock this
place," Calvin says when he sees my
face change. Sam and Henri echo him
as Rhett lights the candle on our table.
"For you," she says. Still, my hand
trembles as I lift a glass of water to my
lips. Flicker-flicker go the lights. Shit.
The reading's about to begin. Why did
I agree to do this? Why did Aguero
have to show? *It's not too late to leave,*
I think, then the professor's by my side.
I stand, shake her hand. "Sorry," I say,
"my hands are ice." Her look says,
Don't worry. I understand. "Word of
advice?" It's not a question. I nod.
"Just honor the poem, Liz. It's not
about you. It's about the work, which
is strong. Do the poem the justice it
deserves, and you'll be fine." As she
walks back to her seat, they call my
name: "First reader up, Liz McLane."
Fifteen feet never felt so freaking far.
As the host raises the mic to my
height, I glance at Rhett, set my poem
on the music stand. No worries, then,
about my shaky hands. Aguero's
words resound in my mind. Warm

against my chest, my charm assures,
I'm near. I clear my throat. "Visiting
Dad's Bench," I hear myself begin:

"I stroke this marble
as if it is your face,
smooth after shaving ... "
The words are there. All I have to do
is believe in them. And not cry.
When I'm done I know I served
that poem well, because all I can hear
is applause.

Last Postcard from Cathy

Amiga,

I don't think this will reach you by 4/1,
but you know I'll be thinking of you
that day. So much has happened in a year!
But how is it possible that a whole year
has passed since your dad died? I'll never
forget that scene at your house after the
funeral—Mrs. W couldn't get over how
you're the tallest in your family, and joked
about your b. father being the cable guy.
I saved you both from calamity, didn't I?
LOL. Anyway, you're on my mind
a ton. Want to hear this song you keep talking
about. Wondering how the search is going.
Your Spanish, too. Language is a fascinating
thing, isn't it? Today Pedro asked about
"bees knees." And how to explain "hot
dog"? Forget "funny bone"—I don't
understand where that comes from, either.
Okay, try to keep smiling, Lizzie, and see
you in two months!

Con amor,
xoxo Cathy

My First (and Last) Date with Sam Paris

It's kind of like driving somebody else's car.
You get behind the wheel (he *does* let you
drive); the seat's back too far, but the thing's
rusted in place, so—you stretch (daintily,
gracefully, you hope) to reach the pedals.
Pedal, that is—you're used to your standard
transmission but this is an automatic. You
know that, but still, your left foot keeps
pumping air (daintily, gracefully, you hope),
feeling for the clutch. Meanwhile, does he
really listen to this station? You can tell
he'd rather you not touch that button. And
whoa—he'd said there was "a bit of body
damage," but didn't warn you about holes
in the floor, about lifting your feet when
splashing through puddles. (So much for
your cute new sandals.) Hey, is there any
heat in this thing? Can we talk? I liked it
in *my* car. I liked it better when we walked.

<u>Scene:</u> **Dorm room, after reading Rhett my "First Date" poem**

Rhett: Was it *that* bad?

Me: Before he dropped his wallet in the puddle, or after I spilled my ten-dollar glass of wine?

Rhett: They let you order *wine?*

Me: It does help being tall. They must have thought twice after we spread those soggy bills all over our table, though. Then, of course, my hands were flying in the air as I told him how Jan and I got to be friends, and I hit my glass—

Rhett: You haven't told me that story.

Me: Oh, third grade—I punched this mean girl—it's best told over a drink.

Rhett: Make mine a Diet Coke today.

Me: Mine, too.

Rhett: And . . . how exactly did your hair get caught in his jacket's zipper?

Me: Don't ask. But—(I pull out a short lock, just barely tucked behind my left ear)—you can guess how we got it out.

Rhett: Ouch. (pause) Did he kiss you?

Me: Like kissing my brother.

Rhett: Double ouch. (pause) I don't suppose there will be a date number two?

Me: We've sworn we'll be better friends than ever. In other words—

Rhett: No.

Me: No. And thanks for not asking what Bob asked. Of course *you* wouldn't. I actually emailed him the poem, because I thought it would crack him up.

(Rhett looks at me quizzically.)

Me (lowering my voice in imitation of Bob): "But I thought you guys took a taxi?" I had to tell him, "It's a *metaphor*, Bob. Driving that car—it's just what the date was *like*."

The Workshop Challenge

(I bring the poem I wrote for the anniversary of Dad's death)

Got up the nerve to bring my "April First"
sestina to workshop. Such an odd thing,
how poets never stop bearing our souls
to strangers. After debating the repetition
of "ok/okay" in the last stanza, Professor
Aguero told us that "When the subject

feels dangerous, form is your friend."
"Liz was born a formalist," remarked
Ben, winking at me over his so-geeky-
they're-cute glasses. "No," said Aguero,
"Liz just works hard." (I winked at Ben
then.) "Classes will be ending in a few

weeks," she went on, "and I hope what
I've been saying about formal verse will
inspire some of you to bring in a sonnet
or pantoum—for better or for worse, just
to try it. Don't worry about it being good.
Worry about knowing how the poem is

made. How that tool in your toolbox
works. Then, when you need it, you'll
be able to reach in and *use* it." Natalia,
who's minoring in film, let out a sigh.
"Who wants to bet her other favorite
pastime is sticking needles in her eyes?"

Journal Entry #2217

Strolling with our cups of tea after workshop, Louise says I've inspired her—she's already been working on a villanelle for more than a week. We try to guess who might take Professor Aguero up on her challenge. Cathy and Colleen will for sure, and Gabe, Von, and Maria. Wren? Maybe. Taylor? Maybe not. Ben? Natalia? A definite no.

"Which reminds me," said Louise, "it's so amazing that Tim was there for you like that the day your father died. No wonder you two are—well, close, still."

I had to explain—he wasn't really. Tim was there the day of the funeral, but it was the sestina's form that led the poem's "speaker" to say it was "today"—the day Dad died.

"So, it wasn't really true?" asked Louise.

"It is here," I said, pointing to my heart.

Confronting Ruth

Not until it's nearly the last
week of classes, Sunday,
do I spot Ruth.

Her guitar's on the bench—she's—what?
She's writing. Left-handed.
She's *left-handed!*

Sam, who's come to the park with me
to sketch, touches my arm.
"Try to be calm."

Sam's right—I don't want Ruth to think
I've turned lunatic while
she was away.

But you know how many people
are left-handed?
Like, ten percent

of the whole world's population.
Sam waits by the fountain
while I breathe deep,

head over to Ruth's bench. "Hey, Ruth,"
I practically whisper,
suddenly shy.

Her rich, brown tan makes her look strong,
healthy, her lengthening
curls are copper

on the ends—sun does that to my
hair, too. Seeing me, Ruth
leaps to her feet—

when she hugs me, I smell sunscreen,
coconut. "Excellent
timing," she says,

"You'll understand this, Liz."
I bet I will, I think.
"It's a hard day,

today. Oh, I'm so extra glad
to see you. Want to sit?"
After moving

her guitar, she motions for me
to join her on the bench.
I want to ask—

to *burst*—but happy as she is
to see me, her eyes are
red and teary.

"This is the anniversary—
ten years today—of my
husband Jack's death."

I open my mouth to say I'm
sorry, but Ruth stops me.
"Too much death, right?"

(Just a cruel fact of life, I guess.)
"Anyway, I'm about
to sing a song—

a song I sang for you once, Liz.
Maybe you'll sing along."
Looking into

the tree tops, Ruth says, "This is for
you, my darling, Jack Smith."
"That was his name?"

I interrupt, my heart beating
like a Congo drum in
Bob Marley's band.

"You were married to Jack? I mean,
you took your husband's name?
Before you were

Ruth Smith you were—" "Ruth Steinberger."
Her turn to interrupt.
She laughs. "Ruth Smith

is a better stage name, don't you
think? But yes—a Jewish
girl from Brooklyn,

that's me. Now, ready to sing, Liz?"
My left hand grabs the bench
under me; my

right rubs my eyes as if something,
suddenly, has stung them.
"Liz, you okay?"

Ruth asks, poised to pluck the first string.
Life's so freakin' crazy.
Ruth Steinberger.

"Yes, I'm fine, Ruth," I say. "Let's sing."
We start: "Although your soul
is full of woe . . ."

Journal Entry #2218

After Ruth and I begin singing, Sam wanders over. He keeps looking at me in a way that I know means he sees something in my face—that something weird has happened—weird for me, at least. *So*, I think, *this is where Reunion Fantasy #2,001 gets me. I had it coming.*

I only stay for that one song. Then I give Ruth a quick hug, say I have to go—she tells me she's going to play "When You Never Said Goodbye" next—and that makes me move all the faster. Still, I keep my head long enough to make sure she won't be alone later today. No one needs to be alone on these anniversaries. She tells me she has plans with friends, and gives me a convincing smile.

Sam, Rhett, Calvin, Henri, Tim, Jan—they only laugh about it now because I do. Ruth Steinberger. Well, I let them all know that I have been told by not one, but *two* Israeli taxi drivers that I look Jewish.

Do I tell Kate & Mom about this when I'm with them on Easter? They'll probably laugh, too.

———

When's the last time I took a nap? When I was five? This afternoon my head feels like cement. I have to lie down. Luckily Rhett is out and the dorm is pretty quiet—I sleep more than two hours. What weird dreams come from daytime sleep.

Birth Mother Letter Dream

Words begin to fail me
teacher, music, siblings
Dear God, how will I do it
I sign the papers Friday

teacher, music, siblings
This writer has always loved
I sign the papers Friday
Don't let her grow up in the city

This writer has always loved
beauty everywhere—nature, poetry
Don't let her grow up in the city
else I'll go on forever

beauty everywhere—nature, poetry—
so many doors are open
else I'll go on forever
blessed with a love of music

So many doors are open
I must put my trust in you
blessed with a love of music
how I'd love to guide her myself

I must put my trust in you
There is much more that could be said
how I'd love to guide her myself
such mental and heartfelt torment

There is much more that could be said
Dear God, how will I do it!
such mental and heartfelt torment
Words begin to fail me

Train Ride, Easter Saturday

It's a light-jacket kind of spring
day when Kate and I take the train
north to Poughkeepsie. Keeper of

crazy hours, Kate sleeps all the way
to Cold Spring. I read Jane Kenyon's
Otherwise, poems published after

she died. She was just forty-seven.
Leukemia. Ruth's husband didn't die
of cancer, but was also taken too

soon—hit by a drunk driver, just after
their honeymoon. *Too much death,*
as Ruth said. And today, the day

before Easter, we mourn Christ in his
tomb. "You look gloomy," says Kate,
yawning. Now that she's awake

I figure I'll fill her in about Ruth,
but she's got stories, too—about
Downtown and Bill the crazy sous-

chef, who makes all the waitresses
cry. We laugh so hard, our mascara
is gone by the time we reach the end

of the line. We spot Mom and Butter
on the platform, wearing matching
polka-dot bandanas. Mom waves;

Butter's tail wags like a wind-shield
wiper gone berserk. "I warned you,"
I whisper, "Our mother is bananas."

Easter Saturday Lunch

(Yet another family meal ruined by yours truly)

Maybe it's the way I bring up Ruth
so casually at first, as if her story will be
like that of Louise and Operation Baby
Powder, or like the one about Rhett and her

brother learning to play gin rummy. Maybe
it's the way I let the story build, filled
with a smoky voice I thought I knew, with
jokes about *Cold Mountain* and Robert Frost,

with the surprise of "Smith," a happy song
when I felt lost, with curly hair, a point on
one ear, and the final twist, left-handedness,
all leading up not to what I'd fantasized

but a Jewish bride from Brooklyn who'd
taken her husband's name, then soon lost
him—but by the time I reach the climax
("Steinberger!"), Mom has Butter's leash

in hand and is rushing for the door. *"No
more,"* warns Kate, and I stop. Butter
looks shocked—he wasn't expecting
a walk when there is Kate's chowder

and salmon on the table and what smells
like cheesecake for dessert. He hasn't
even finished the chewy Mom had tossed
him when we'd sat down. Now she is

running out the door, her face a cross
between grizzly-bear and shipwreck.
"She'll be back," Kate says with a frown.
I just stare at Mom's empty chair.

Mom Returns from Her Surprise Walk with a Determined Look on Her Face

Elbows on the table,
head in my hands,
I sit in silence while
the chowder turns
cold. Kate picks
at her salad. For half
an hour the clock
ticks and we don't
say boo. By quarter
to one, Mom and Butter
come back, Butter full
of wags and half-
chewed-chewy-nut-
rapture. Mom full of—
what? Not annoyance.
Purpose? She sits
down with us, says,
"Lizzie, for years
you've had these
fantasies about finding
your birth mother.
They have filled me
with worries that
you'll have your
heart broken, because
it seemed that it might
never happen. But
now, perhaps, it will.
You're *so close*—
soon, I think, you'll
meet her. So listen.
I'm not going to say
this as some token
sermon of wisdom,
or to keep you from

dreaming about
what that day will
be like. I might
as well ask you
to stop breathing."
(Am I breathing?
I'm glad for
the reminder.)
"Just—try hard
to remember two
things: one, she loves
you very deeply.
Keep that always
in your heart.
Because two,
she's as human
as the rest of us.
Don't anoint her
to some kind of
sainthood, because
then she's bound
to disappoint."

After Church: Easter Sunday Brunch, Then Back to the New York-Bound Train

"Let's call Bob before you head back—he must
be up by now," Mom says as our waiter
slides the bill onto our table. When her
train was leaving last night, Kate said, "I trust
at brunch tomorrow, you'll praise those who must
cook all those fried eggs and omelets on Easter
Sunday, and rise at dawn, unlike our brother
who'll sleep 'til noon." When I tell Bob, he busts
up over that. "Hey, tell her I was up by nine!"
he says. Mom, who's now driving, winks. "Ask him
which time zone." It's good for Mom and me
to laugh. So I pull out my journal. "Mind
if I read you my 'First and Last Date' with Sam
poem?" "Only," Mom says, "if it's funny."

Good News While Studying in the Park

My phone starts to play "Winter River," so
I know it's Tim. Can't help myself—why not
talk with him? On Ruth's bench, a sparrow

stands alert. "She's in the country, where you
should be," I tell the bird. "I'd rather be
in New York City," says Tim. "Well, you blew

that, going to school in Florida, then
getting yourself a cute girlfriend," I tease,
then add, "Hi, Tim. Really, how've you been?

Thanks for the Easter text." Tim hesitates.
"Well. Yeah. I'm good. But my golf clubs aren't,"
he says mysteriously. "But here's great

news—Zeena and I have . . . well, parted ways."
That *is* great news, but I wonder why he
thinks so. "That tournament, Easter Sunday?

She was in the lead. Then totally blew
it. Threw a little hissy fit right there
on the green. I told her I never knew

she was such a bad sport. This was later,
in the parking lot. That's when she busted
my clubs with her car. She's an alligator—

Landon always said so." "That's a bummer
about your clubs, though," I say. "She paid me,"
he says. ". . . Think I could visit this summer?"

Journal Entry #2219

<u>Scene:</u> **Louise & I waiting in line for tea at the Third Rail**

Louise asks if my mother expects presents on Mother's Day (no, just a phone call, which I already made, I tell her, leaving out how Mother's Day is always a loaded subject). Apparently, her mother demands *gifts* (plural) and hers weren't up to par.

Then she tells me that Kimiko isn't coming back this fall. She's actually transferring to community college back in Arizona. Louise is looking everywhere—the menu board, the window, at people drinking tea and coffee at the little wood tables—but not at me. I can tell she's trying not to cry. I tell her not to worry—Bob went to community college and immediately after got swept up by this software company in Silicon Valley. Kate says he'll probably be a millionaire someday, and never have a BA or have to pay a college loan. I explain how it turns out that our brother is brilliant—he's already got a patent! Who knew? So maybe Kimiko will do well, too.

Louise: Well, Kimiko could be brilliant. But I'm not sure she's *that* brilliant. She is good company, though.

Me: But you'll be back this fall.

Louise: Yeah, but I might have to live at home. Kimiko's actually my cousin—she was the reason my parents let me stay on campus. They won't pay for it now.

Me (thinking: *I am so lucky.*): You could still hang with me, with us—

Louise (stops): Liz, you are such a nice person. You know that? Naïve, but nice.

Me: Not so bad for a country girl?

. . . she hugged me.

On the walk home from class, I spot Ruth in the park. I haven't seen her since Passover, which coincided this year with Easter. She's writing something in a little blue notebook, then stopping to strum her guitar. Hating when people interrupt me if I'm writing, I decide to leave her be— but she sees me, waves me over.

She is so inquisitive about my weekend at home for Easter that I decide to tell her ALL, my _whole_ story, right through the Steinberger punch line. "Oh, Liz, I'm so flattered," she says, laughing so hard little tears spring from her eyes. A knot in my stomach unravels. I laugh, too.

Frustrating realization: I ask why she plays guitar right-handed. "Because no one would teach me left-handed," she says, and I think, WHOA. If I hadn't been so stubborn, I could have learned that way, too . . . I would be a good player by now.

According to Ruth, "When You Never Said Goodbye" was one of Jessica Rose Hemley's hits, but it was actually written by Hemley's friend, Iona Grosart. Ruth doesn't know if Grosart was adopted, but that's my guess. As for "mother-ghost," Ruth thinks it means dead, like the mother died suddenly without having a chance to say goodbye. That makes me think of Ruth's husband, and Tim—how he lost his mother when he was a baby. He's going to love this song. Maybe this summer he'll hear Ruth play. . .

"Let's sing it together, okay?" Ruth says, lifting her guitar to her lap. I nod. My voice is a whisper when we begin, but grows bolder by the second verse. Then I'm lost in it all—wind-blown, sea-borne. Ruth winks.

———

. . . I just texted Karen Mason. Told her please, _please_ don't text, email, or call me, no matter _what_, until after exams end on May 17. It's hard enough focusing without her asking me to call Sophie at The Foundling, or telling me—anything else.

Need I Say More?

(Two Haiku in Honor of NYU's Annual Strawberry Festival)

1)

Ten-thousand berries / sweeten New York's best,
longest,
strawberry shortcake

2)

We eat strawberry
ice cream, smoothies,
cheese
beneath
strawberry balloons

Coffee Study Break With One of Us Five Missing

Rhett swears she smells coffee. Then: knock knock—
knock knock. Henri? This wasn't the plan originally;
I was heading to the library, but Rhett convinced me
we could study here. When the clock struck one, Sam,
Calvin, and Henri would show. We'd have chocolate,
a box of Fig Newtons. The boys would bring coffee.
So here's Sam and Calvin with a crock-pot of French
roast. They even brought soy milk for me. But
where's Henri? A few minutes later, my phone ding-
dongs. "Don't wait 4 me," reads Henri's text. "Maybe
c u at the rock friday. Good luck w/ rest of classes
& finals & hi to the tribe!" "What's up with that?"
Calvin asks, his arm around Rhett. Can't he guess?

Metaphor Poem for Last Workshop: "Studying for Final Exams"

Got my hiking
boots, back-
pack, walking
stick. Got
a water bottle,
trail mix,
map. Now
it's straight
up
this
mountain
of memory—
these tests
of all
I know—
until
I reach
the patch
on top
where
blueberries
grow

One Chapter Closes, Another Opens on Its Heels

As crowded as a subway car at rush hour, Mind of Snow
barely audible above the din, cellar-dark and smelling
of sweat and beer, The Rock is clearly the place to be for
an end-of-finals party. Rhett and Calvin made it here early
enough to grab a table—Sam's here now, too, and we four
toast this day. "Think you did okay?" shouts Rhett, already
a little tipsy. I smile, lift my drink in reply, then glance
around for Henri. "Hey!" calls Sam, who sees her first—
she spots him waving one arm. Calvin and Rhett squish
over to make room for her to sit. But wait. She's not alone.
Henri elbows her way over to us, her face brighter than
the candle Rhett just lit. "Hey, guys, this is Edmund,"
she says, "Edmund Dante Rodriguez." Calvin knows him—
I think Sam, too—they rise, shake his hand. "Edmund
Dante?" Rhett yells, looking like Henri just said "free
drinks." The guy looks familiar. "Like, the Count of Monte
Christo?" Rhett's standing now, ready to hug him. A storm
cloud rushes across Henri's face. Edmund makes a low bow.
"Wow! My favorite book of all time!" Rhett squeals like
a kid. Putting my hand on Henri's arm, I feel her relax.
"My mother's, too," says Edmund. He slides his arm around
Henri's waist; out pops the sun again. "A round of drinks?
We're heading for the bar," Edmund offers. As I dig through
my purse for some cash, I realize I have a text I didn't hear.
Then the roar of people, the music, my friends next
to me, fade. It's as if I'm under water. The text is from
Karen Mason: "Tests done? Been sitting on your info two
days. Call when you get this." I stare at those words.
My heart thumps harder than the band's base beat bouncing
off the walls. My mouth's cardboard. Will my legs hold if I
stand? "I can cover you 'til later," Henri's saying in my
ear. "We know you're good for it," Edmund adds, as if
I didn't hear. "Liz, why do you look so weird?" asks Rhett.
Their voices sound so far away. "No—thanks," I manage
to say. "Something's come—up. I really have to go."

After the Text

I remember trembling
out on the sidewalk

as if it were snowing
and I had no coat,

but don't remember
leaving The Rock.

I remember Karen
saying "complicated"

and "Mark 'Saturday
delivery,'" but don't

recall what else she
said, or what was so

"complicated" at all.
I remember Rhett

walking me to UPS,
her endless chatter

to ease the stress, but
have no memory of

first fetching the money
order from our room.

I do remember sending
the money. Soon after,

hugging Rhett, hailing
a cab. The ride over

is fuzzy: I can't picture
letting myself in Kate's

apartment door, or
texting Kate to say

I was there. Ginger
tea, I remember that;

me calling Mom,
insisting, *No, don't*

come. I remember Tim
playing his guitar

into the phone, but
I'm not sure when

Kate got home. Garlic
and mint: her scent

as she hugged me.
Her voice was a balm

to the wound we were
born with, for the grief

we've always carried
for something that was

ruptured, something
torn then hidden away

long before we had our
say in our own futures.

There was no use in
even trying to sleep.

It's all been leading
to this day, I recall

thinking as Kate and I
watched the sun rise.

The sun. It was fat
and red as a beach ball

over Brooklyn. Yes,
I remember that.

Waiting for Karen's Email, Thinking,
"A New Road Beneath Me"

Soon after dawn I finally slept,
        dreamless—

then woke,
        feeling a new road beneath me.

Life has taken
        another turn—

this one just as sharp
        but different

from the turn Dad's death
        made, and the road

I've now found myself on
        is a road

I've always dreamed of driving

Journal Entry #2221

I wake to the smell of eggs and coffee. Dressed in Kate's sweats, my hair a tangled nest, I'm practically richocheting off the walls like a pinball. Karen said she'd send the email by 10 a.m. I glance at the clock—less than an hour until then.

"When You Never Said Goodbye" is on eternal replay in my mind, haunting me:

> Had that dream again of asters
> and black birds—you like a page torn—
> just outside my door.
> The wind stirs
> and the leaves all let go.
> Rushed out to greet you,
> your face turned to snow.

After one look at me in the little kitchen's doorway, Kate says, "For you, I'm brewing half decaf. You've already got the jitters." Or the shivers. I can't seem to warm up.

Kate sets up her laptop on the coffee table near the couch while I shower. At 9:55, the email flashes in my inbox:

"Dear Liz, are you in a place where you can speak privately? If so, please call me asap. Thanks, Karen."

This wasn't expected.

Karen's Call (On Speaker Phone)

"I have to admit I've been grateful for
the extra few days to think this through,"
Karen says when I call. "Your case is more
unusual than any other—this is new
to me, and I thought it best to explain
on the phone." Beside me on the couch, Kate
takes my hand. "In order to save you pain,
I've made a few calls. Liz, to tell you straight—
this isn't the *best* news." "Oh my God she's dead!"
I blurt. "No, no, not that—she's very much alive,"
Karen says, "and it's important I add ahead
of time that she's so happy to know *you're* alive
and well. . . . She'll send you a letter. Only one.
Liz, I'll just say it: your mother is a nun."

No Joke: One Might Say She's "Taken"

Like when I learned that Dad was dead,
I thought it was a joke. What's the punch
line that follows, "Your mother is a nun"?

Unfortunately, there isn't one. After all
my day dreams, even Rhett's jokes,
I never for a minute thought—well,

it doesn't matter now what I thought.
This isn't my fantasy; this isn't a hoax.
Out of all the stories under the sun, this

is one I didn't think *happened* any more—
this felt like some black and white movie
or that old novel Mom loves, *Mariette*

in Ecstasy. But three years after I was
born, my first mother entered the Sisters
of the Joyful Resurrection. First she was

a novice, then took her final vows. Karen
said she did some "fancy dancing," but
she's convinced them—the nun in charge—

to let my mother write me one letter.
That's all. As Mother Superior reportedly
put it, "She is married to Jesus now."

Refusing the Urge to Go Numb

I.
Suddenly I feel cold
again, this time, cold
to my core: a chill
that begins with my
innermost cell, that
cell a seed sprouting
with ill omens,
promising nothing
but numbness. I sense
a trembling, deep
and wordless.

II.
But—wait. Say No
to that, NO.
Look beside you.
Here is your sister,
Kate. Would you
have had your fate
turn any other way?
Your birth mother
gave you a gift.
Gifts—who reside
in your heart. This
heart, now growing
luminous,
warm to the touch.

Journal Entry #2222

Kate googles "Sisters of the Joyful Resurrection." Their website knocks us out. It's so . . . professional, easy to navigate, packed with facts about this religious order, a site geared toward both "lay people" like us and women who think they might be interested in joining. And many do. Ninety-two sisters reside at the convent in Oregon. Their average age: THIRTY. Young nuns in the 21st century!

"Who knew?" Kate says, shaking her head. Most of them enter the convent when they're 25 or 26, and the majority have college degrees.

"Do you think God really 'calls' you?" I ask Kate. "I mean, not on the phone! But, does He whisper in you ear? Kick you under the table? Nudge your elbow?"

Kate's still glued to her laptop screen. "They're a 'semi-cloistered' order."

Setting down my cold mug of decaf, I realize my hand is shaking. "What's that mean?"

Kate googles the term. Reads: "'The semi-cloistered community separates themselves partially from the world, in that their members do not go out into the world to work, but bring those in need into their houses. They will have schools or orphanages, etc. but inside their communities. Whatever apostolate they have takes place inside their community with the people coming to them and leaving.'"

My head's thrumming, as if I've had too many shots of Pineapple Bombers. We study every photo on the convent's website, trying to pick out my birth mother's face despite the brown and white habits that hide their hair and pretty much everything else. The only nuns I "know" are the ones I've seen in church all my life. They sit together, four or five of them, in the front pew. They're old (older than Mom) and don't wear habits—I guess nuns don't have to anymore if they don't want to—but their long, navy wool skirts and starched white blouses are kind of like uniforms. And of course they all wear crosses around their necks. Wooden ones, smaller than the crosses the altar servers wear. They teach in New Hook's

Catholic School, but what else do they do? Pray the rest of the day? I've never thought about it. Here on this website we see nuns walking side by side on woodsy paths; nuns gardening; nuns standing before smart boards, teaching a classroom full of children; nuns playing *basketball*. What stuns us most is how they're not only all so young, they're also all smiling. Real, honest-to-goodness smiles. Maybe life is less complicated when you don't have a boyfriend. Or a husband.

"I think she's happy," I say. I lean on Kate. She rubs my back as I finally give in to this wave that's pulling me under, roaring in my ear—*Semi-cloistered. You will never meet her.*

Kate Texts Bob, Who Sets Up a Family Conference Call

How to weigh the silence wafting from Kate's phone?
With patience, I hear Dad say, *because they are*
as shocked as you. "Thank God you weren't alone

when you got this news," says Mom. "No wonder,"
says Bob, "Your favorite movie was *The Sound*
of Music." "You promised *no* jokes," Kate says under

her breath. "Bob," scolds Mom, "*really?* Sometimes!"
"It's okay. I do love that movie," I say. "But my favorite
is *It's a Wonderful Life,* and I don't have to see mine

erased to appreciate what I've got." "Yeah, well, *see,*"
says Bob, "she hasn't lost her sense of humor."
"And now, admit it," I add, "you're *all* relieved."

Journal Entry #2223

So much for believing in my bones that my birth mother was here, in the city. Karen, now the intermediary between the Prioress General (also known as "Mother Superior") and me, says I'll have my letter soon.

"Don't expect a lot," Karen warns when she calls again. "It will be short. And you can't respond. In a semi-cloistered order like your mo—your birth mother's—a person's whole focus is supposed to be—well, on God. And her community, her fellow sisters, and their work. They run some kind of school in a pretty poor area. Anyway she's taken these vows, and one of them is obedience . . . I guess that means she has to do what the boss, the Prioress, thinks is best, without questioning it."

Kate puts her arm around me. I'm out of words.

"Liz," Karen says, sensing it's a good time to change the subject, "I don't imagine you've looked at the names and addresses I emailed to you? I know you have a lot to absorb!"

(You can say that again.) "No."

"Okay, then—you must know that your grandmother died a few years ago. I'm sorry." *(Any other sucky news, Karen?)* "And for some reason, they're not telling your grandfather that you've made contact. I think they want to keep this quiet, let it go—well, dormant again. But you'll see, when you are ready to look at the information I sent you, that you have two aunts and an uncle, and they have children—meaning you have first cousins . . . you can look them up. When you're ready for that. No one can stop you."

Kate looks at me like, "Will you?" I just shrug. Maybe. In time.

————

Now I feel dumb for thinking my birth mother was some famous writer—that she'd sacrificed me for her muse. I guess she sacrificed me for God instead. Who can argue with that?

Jan can, that's who. She cursed like a pirate when I filled her in. "But Lizzie gets a letter—that's more than I ever got," said Jade. That shut up Jan. But when they offered to come down, I hesitated—then said no. I blamed Writers in NY, though that's not starting for two days. I guess I really just can't handle Jan's anger right now. She's maybe madder than I am at that Mother Superior. At the whole situation.

One website Kate found, from the Daughters of the Immaculate Heart of Mary, helped to explain a lot. It says that a woman enters a convent because her love of Jesus is so deep, she can't do anything else. It's the kind of love that makes you sacrifice everything—your nice clothes, your make-up ... all of your "stuff," plus your parents and brothers and sisters and friends. They don't say, "and your child," but I guess that would fall under "everything."

————

Rhett and Henri are kicking themselves for not applying to Writers in NY— the summer program would have meant four more weeks together. "We hate to leave you *now!*" says Rhett as she folds her black and white dress.

"Just when maybe you need us *most,*" adds Henri, helping box up Rhett's books, which I promised to ship to her parents' house in Greensboro. That's how she sent most of her stuff home. Henri's already packed, and mailed her boxes home to Boston last week.

I know they mean it about wanting to stay, but suspect maybe more they regret leaving Calvin and Edmund—and Sam, too. I assure them that I'll be fine, and remind them we'll be talking on Facebook and Skype or on the phone.

Plus I have Kate. Tim will be here in five days. And next week, Cathy, too. I'm hoping Ruth will be back before then—she's down in Florida for her father's birthday.

Still, I couldn't help but cry when Rhett and Henri left. Their hugs felt like some kind of sentence: *You will always wind up alone.*

Grounded: Twenty Minutes After Rhett & Henri Head Home

(Inspired by a few more feathers flown out of my old pillow)

I feel like the lone goose left in the north
after my flock has flown south for winter—
except it's nearly summer and clearly
my friends have scattered in every direction.
Before he left, Sam stopped by one more
time to say goodbye. It seemed that he had
more to say than that, but he let those words

lie. He did tell me he'd spotted someone
who looked like Ruth on St. Mark's Place—
still, it's not until I spy her face in the park
that I'll believe such good news. She did
text from Florida to check on me—she says
she's writing songs again, says I'm her
inspiration; I've become her muse.

One Hour Later: Unmoored

Goose, geese—who am I kidding?
Stop. No use calling this what it's
not. I'm a dinghy adrift in the sea
of my birth mother's refusal. About
to be wrecked in the tsunami
of her rejection. Upon reflection,
that's what it is, right? For once
in her life, couldn't she take a chance,
disobey, break the rules—for *me?*
Mom and Kate say No, that's how
it is when a nun takes a vow. So
now I say, *Screw it. Screw her,*
with a punch to my pillow. Like
a puff of steam, a few feathers
spew into the air. WHAM—I slam
that pillow against the wall—
WHAM that pillow calls me FOOL
for all my silly daydreams JERK
for all the years and years of waiting
WHAM my stupid hopes WHAM
(feathers everywhere) WOMP
I hope I look like him and not her
WHAM how dare she make me
think she cared WOMP I'll burn
that letter just like Jan WHACK!
FORGET HER! WHAM!

Coughing, I hack up feathers, sink
to my knees. *"This isn't how it's
supposed to be—"* My voice
a whisper now. *"Please, mother—
all I ever wanted—please
don't say no. Don't go away
again. Not again."* I cough into
the pillow, grip it with both hands
as if it's a life preserver. *"Shit!*

I don't understand! . . . Or I do.
All my bad dreams were true."

. . . Did someone say something?
What—what's that? A hand on my
arm, a voice saying gently, "Liz."
I swing around to see Rhett's look
of alarm. *Rhett's back?* Rhett,
with one arm around me, the other
swatting at the cloud that hovers
in the air. Her eyes are red, cheeks
look hot. I let the pillow drop.
A loud moan escapes me. Rhett
pulls a feather from my hair.
Now I see someone else is here,
standing behind Rhett. She wears
a teary, frightened smile. Henri.

Rhett & Henri to the Rescue

They'd shared a cab, got as far
as LaGuardia. Split the fare.
Then stood there on the sidewalk. Stared at each other for a full
ten seconds. Then ran
as fast as their roller-bags would
let them to the end of the taxi
line. Only twelve or thirteen
people were ahead of them—
they'd be back to Goddard by
four. As they waited, Henri
whipped out her cell, called
the woman at NYU—Ms.
Flynn—they knew Ms. Flynn
would understand, let them
stay another week—and she
did. Their parents, too.
Twenty minutes later they
crossed the Williamsburg
Bridge. Slapped a high-five
as they zipped into Manhattan.
I didn't ask why they came
back. It's what friends do.
It's what true friends do.

We Three (Henri, Rhett, & Me)

We're the Three Musketeers,
Three Little Bears,
Three Stooges, too

We are a tripod,
a triad, we are
red, white, and blue

We're a three-piece suit,
we're three of a kind,
we are *in* 3-D

We're the *Niña*,
the *Pinta*,
and the *Santa María*

We're the Brontë sisters,
the three feet in a yard,
and three sheets to the wind

(when we've had more
than
enough)

We're a tricycle,
a triangle,
the Billy Goats Gruff

We're three French Hens,
a three-ring circus,
we're a theater, popcorn, and a movie starring us

My Mind, That Hive, Buzzes with Memories. . . Wonders: What Next?

I remember picnics with Peter at James Bard State Park,
dances in a gym, candles' flames, a silver charm on its chain,
our family portrait, home games, girls crossing their hearts in the dark.
I remember carriage rides, high fives, Kate's chowder;
Bob, that furry bear; new school shoes, poems as a cure for the blues,
adoption taboos, and Dad placing a log on the fire.
I remember phone call stories, Canada geese, the Broken Place;
Kate stirring chili, Mom stirring paint, tongues dyed blue on Parents' Night;
a poem of longing, a window closing, believing we're mistakes.
I remember Jan fixing cars (her father, too), Cathy twirling her braids;
matters of loyalty, a hurt little bird, Peter's imaginary key;
faces on the street, whispered words, the playground in third grade.

I remember spiked lemonade, feeling betrayed, dancing the Dip-Doo;
Tim's arms around me, Kate saying I'm pretty, Reunion Fantasy #1003,
train rides to the city, Sharon and Jackie, Jan's rainbow of hair-dos.
I remember adoption registries; that Broken Place again, a marble bench,
a friendship's end, singing "Amazing Grace" as they buried my father;
"Hello, Cards 'n Gifts!," Mom standing stiff, learning I'm Scottish and
French.
I remember postcards from Mexico, a teacher's note, the knowledge of
crows;

Gertie's Diner (no omelets are finer!), a mess of a girl in a mirror;
German potato salad, me flipping my lid, my metal stool at Mack's Auto.
I remember a hobo's crouch, Mom curled on the couch, unable to paint;
my charm gone missing, saying "No" too late, a night in Dad's car,
bonfires and hangovers, a fridge full of leftovers, George stealing cake.

I remember crazy suitemates; a packed car, Butter in the back seat;
the Pigeon-Man shuffle, Mom's feathers ruffled, country-girl handshakes;
The Rock before four o'clock, Kin Solvers (Rhett's reminder to breathe).
I remember Dad's empty chair, dogs at the shelter, Ruth tuning her guitar;
Henri with those cookies, Sam sketching me, Louise and tea and poetry;
dumplings at Klong, a walk with Kate in East River Park.

I remember baby powder, Rhett singing in the shower, Calvin brewing

coffee;

Scrabble and wine, Karen's kind voice, the open mic, birthday cards on

fire;

Sophie's gray eyes, "How to Change a Tire," striking out at the library.
I remember Ruth in her black hat, all-night chats, "Smith," and Tim pulling

back,

popcorn, snowshoes, Jan and Jade's calls, Sam's soggy wallet,
Rhett quoting Eliot, Bob's wise cracks, that live letter in my backpack.

. . . now another letter is on its way. At last, my first mother will have her say.

Fine

(Day before the Writers in New York Program begins)

Tomorrow my Writers in New York class will walk
the Brooklyn Bridge, read Whitman and Hart Crane
while the East River flows below. Rhett and Henri
know I won't be alone, so have plans of their own—
window shopping in SoHo, a street fair near Madison
Square Park. I decide to silence my phone—Mom
and Kate are busy, and Bob and Tim and Jan and Jade
can leave me a voicemail, or send a text (they all call
constantly; I've made a game of guessing who will
be next). "Thanks, but I'm fine, I'm fine," I keep
insisting. "Yes," says Mom, "you will be. In time."

Journal Entry #2224: The Promised Letter

(It's in my mailbox when I get back from the Brooklyn Bridge; glad Rhett & Henri are still out, I read it in my dorm room.)

My Dear Elizabeth,

How I have longed to say those words. Every day since I signed the papers of relinquishment more than 18 years ago, I have prayed that I would have the chance someday to say to you what is in my heart. I'm so grateful that God has offered me this chance. God, I should say, and your steadfast spirit.

Because it's been decided that it's best we do not meet, I have been allowed to speak not only with Karen Mason, but with Sophie Fedorowicz at The Foundling. It's through Sophie that I've learned what a kind, intelligent, and accomplished young woman you've turned out to be. That you are a poet comes as no surprise, as your grandmother was a poet—were she alive, she'd be as happy and proud as I am to know you've followed in her footsteps. (Your grandfather—my father—is alive but very frail since Mom died. I must agree it's best we not tell him about your finding me.)

All I've ever wanted for myself was to know you were safe and happy. Learning that you have been blessed with the loving, caring parents I'd hoped for has filled me with immeasurable solace and such *great* happiness. My friend, Sister Francesca, says I no longer walk, but float. I tell you this to dispel any lingering doubts you may have about my love for you, dear Lizzie. (Sophie says your family calls you that. I hope you don't mind if I do, too. It does seem like a miracle that you've kept the name I gave you. All the first-born girls in the Smith clan are named Elizabeth.) I wish I were able to send you more than one letter, but must be grateful for this much. I will do my best to explain what could otherwise take decades.

Having grown up in Catholic schools on Long Island (Kings Park), I often felt close to the nuns who were my teachers. I didn't realize I was meant to be one myself until I turned 13—it was then that instead of boys, God came calling. My parents were surprised. When they realized this desire was not a passing fancy, they worried about "losing" their youngest child behind convent walls. They convinced me to go to college before making up my mind.

I won't go into everything that happened that first year at NYU. *You* happened. Just know that you were conceived in what I thought was love. When that fantasy dissolved, I clung to you, growing inside me. I told myself that I would let go of my dream; I would still be a teacher, but not a nun. We would be a family. My mother let me think things through. My father was less than happy. Oh, Lizzie, how I prayed those months before and after you were born. There was so much I wanted to give you. Finally I knew—to give you that, I must give you up. That was like losing a limb. And like an amputee who still feels her missing arm or leg, I have always felt your presence, always felt that pain of loss. But when at last I knew what I had to do for you, I also knew what I had to do for me. To respect my parents, I finished college. By that time, God was knocking loudly on my heart's door! When I took my vows, I understood you had been God's first gift to me. By listening to Him, I was given another. And now, this news of you—what a priceless treasure!

Sophie tells me that *you* are a student at NYU. I like to think some essence of us lingers there, and that's what drew you to that school. How many hours I sat in Washington Square Park, singing softly to soothe you when I felt you turn or kick. The park was often filled with people playing music, no matter what the weather. Now I will picture you there—from Sophie's description, I know you very much resemble me. (I have no photo to send you, but if you visit our website, you'll see me in our garden, staking peas. In another photo, Sister Francesca is holding a basketball, and I'm in the background with my hands in the air. I hold the record for most free-throws in a row!)

Because Karen already has gathered so much information, I'm putting together a little family tree to help you make sense of it all. I will be able to send this to you through her. My sisters and brother know about you. (They have from the beginning.) If you ever feel like contacting them, I'm sure they will be happily surprised, and *welcoming*. Your cousins, too. I believe that they will all be proud to know *you* are their relative, Elizabeth Ann McLane. Since you look so much like me, I imagine they will also know who you are at first sight!

Before I close, I have to tell you—I sought out a semi-cloistered community. It was part of my calling—I don't expect you to understand. Some days I'm still trying to understand it myself. But these last few days have certainly thrown me into a whirlwind of emotion, making it hard for me to focus on my purpose here. Perhaps that's why Sister Gabriella (our Prioress General) made the decision she did. It's not for me to question.

All I ask is that if you don't understand, you at least *try* to accept who I am. And, if you need to, please forgive me? Acceptance, forgiveness, love—they are the only path toward happiness (another name for God).

How to end this letter, when I could go on for years? With a prayer that you'll be safe, healthy, and happy. And that you will know you were always wanted, always loved.

> Blessings and peace
> be yours forever,
>
> Sister Dorothy
> your first mother

p.s.

It's so very difficult to say hello and then goodbye. Please realize that every time you wake, every time you glance in the mirror, chances are I'm praying for *you*.

I've Read that Letter Twice & Don't Know What to Feel

...the road beneath me
has changed again. No—
it hasn't turned left
or right, not become
a new road, exactly.
Instead, there's
a difference in the light.
I've moved from murk
to rain. A shower, really;
I can see, but I'm afraid
to be happy or sad or
anywhere between.
It's not anything I can
yet explain to Kate
who's at work or Mom,
who's planting flowers
at Dad's grave. So instead,
I run down seven flights
of stairs, burst through
the turnstile and Goddard's
front door, then cross
the street to the park.
This park I've visited
since I was in the womb.
I know, *I know* she'll be
here. And she is. Ruth.
Ruth's kind eyes darken,
sense the rain falling
inside me. We talk—
I talk—and then I read.
And reading that letter,
I hear Mom's voice:
*The universe is unfolding
as it should.* Ruth puts
her hand in mine. "Liz,

we've had enough
of grief," she says when
I'm done. "*This* is yet
another gift: your other
mother's words and what
you now know. There's
nothing left to do but
believe. You're no longer
stranded out at sea."

First Mother: So Near, Yet So Far

So much like Dad's death, this
could take years to absorb,
to accept. I take it in as a swimmer
takes a breath, then keep
kicking, keep
pulling through this water's
murky depths.

Journal Entry #2225

She *is* a mother-ghost.

Or, a ghost mother:
here, and yet not
here.

What Might Have Been

In daydreams
I am the ghost
peering into windows
of what might have been.
Look, there in the glow
of my parents' kitchen
I'm sitting at the table
sipping tea. Across
from me is a woman—
her eyes, my own
brown earth. Her hands
reach out for mine—

and now we're arm
in arm, strolling
through the park.
People passing say,
"How tall they are!
They look so much alike!"
And they are right.
We smile, wave at Ruth,
who's playing our song.
My heart opens
like a door. So we sit
for a while. *Listen,*
she says, *to my story.*
Then, tell me yours.

Journal Entry #2226

Every time I glance at these photographs, newly framed on the little table next to my bed, I'm startled. It's like jumping at your own shadow, then realizing, *Oh—it's just me.*

But the woman in these photos is *not* me. And—what's really starting to sink in—she's not a ghost, either. Thanks to the convent's website, I have not just one photo, but two of her—this first mother I've fantasized about my entire life.

1) Her ginger-brown habit blends in with the garden she's kneeling in, as a deer blends into the forest. Her profile makes me do a double take—there is the incline of my own nose; there is the slight upward curl of my lips, as if I'm happy but not quite smiling. Yet most of all, I stare at her hands. Those long fingers grasping a thin wood pole and the sort of green mesh that Gram used to stake her peas. Now I know who to thank for my fingers—and, I'm guessing, my toes—that, years ago, I compared to root vegetables God pulled from a garden.

2) This one completely slays me. In my high school year book, there's a photo of me striking this exact pose at a home game: Margaret Dunn is in the foreground; I'm a few feet back, my hands raised above my head, mouth slightly open. Just like my birth mother. Like my other mother, this tall woman who plays basketball *and* went to NYU.

When I catch myself staring at that face, I think, *That's not you. But— someday, you'll look just like that.* What a strange feeling. As if she's put her arm around my shoulders. Then I hear her words: "Every time you wake, every time you glance in the mirror, chances are I'm praying for you."

Happy tears. These, running down my face, are mostly happy tears.

Mom & I Have the Longest Talk Ever

... and now I feel like a traveler
who's been driving and driving

for years
not always paying attention

when she steers
or missing the signs, often lost

and surprised by those turns
they call "blind,"

but who suddenly
brakes

because she realizes
HEY, I know that house

I just passed—I know this road
that I'm on—

I know where I am!
I'm home. Home at last.

Journal Entry #2227

Goals for the rest of summer & coming year:

1) Read more, write more, drink less.
2) Have a long, face-to-face, heart-to-heart talk with Tim. Are we together, or not? And if we are, what does that mean?
3) Practice reading in public—go to as many open mics as possible.
4) Learn to play guitar. Ruth says she'll teach me. Left-handed.
5) Take a song-writing class . . . writing lyrics could be a blast.
6) Send copies of *The Secret of Me* and *The Girl in the Mirror* to my birth mother, to Sister Dorothy at her convent in Oregon. Maybe they'll let her read them. They said no letters, but they didn't say no book manuscripts. At least I'll have tried to communicate—to tell her what it's been like to be me. To let her know that she did the right thing. That giving me up—it turned out okay. More than okay. She gave me a wonderful life.

Charmed

This silver full moon around my neck
lights my way through dark and broken

places, illuminates the faces of those
I love—faces around the dinner table,

on the other end of the phone. Faces
that let me know I'm not alone—

faces framed by wild dark braids
and hot-pink spikes; freckled faces,

olive faces, cocoa-brown faces
and once-pale faces now browned

by sun. Even a new face, one that
mirrors my own, peeking out

from a white cloth called a wimple.
I've stared at that mirror for a long,

long time. Its reflection, like its love,
is not a simple one. But it's mine.

A Haiku: I Swear Before You and God Above

My one and true name:
Elizabeth Ann McLane,
lucky daughter of

Like a Tree

Sometimes I'm dizzy with it all—Dad dead
and first mother a nun, the fear that love

will chose another if I'm not good enough.
But how lucky I was, as Mom said,

to have had such a father; and the love
of my first mother was so very deep,

like the roots of a tree, that even when
she gave her greatest gift, those roots held tough—

still hold me. Love isn't something to keep,
after all, but to give away. And love,

I've learned, is like a special tree. In storms it bends
but does not break. Its blossoms lure the bees.

Each year it grows another ring where none was.
What's not true love burns bright, then falls like leaves.

The Story Behind the Novel

READERS OFTEN ASK ME, "Is Lizzie McLane really *you?*" I have to explain that no, she is a fictional character who "lives" only in my imagination. I do like to add that Lizzie is the teenager I wish I had been. At least, I wish I had been as brave as she is when I was young, as determined to speak my mind and to express my feelings in poems, if not out loud.

Like Lizzie, I am adopted. But I wasn't writing poems about that when I was fourteen, as Lizzie does in the first book I wrote about her, *The Secret of Me*. While I started writing poems when I was about twelve, adoption was a subject I avoided on paper and in most conversations until I was in my mid-twenties. And though I lost my dad at a fairly early age—twenty-six—my second book about Lizzie, *The Girl in the Mirror*, tells of her losing her father when she's only a senior in high school. Still, losing my dad rocked my world much the way Lizzie's father's death rocks hers.

In this third book Lizzie, or "Liz," as she is now known, searches for her birth mother—which I also did, but it took me until I was twenty-eight to begin.

Yet we *do* have a great deal in common, Liz and I.

Like Liz, I spent the first five months of my life in foster care. Until that point, my birth mother had hesitated to sign the papers that would mean surrendering me and making me available for adoption. She wanted to raise me. She wanted me to have a life filled with love and with opportunities. She believed that, "So many doors are open to the mind that is filled with the beauty to be found everywhere—in nature, poetry, music. The person who is out to learn all that is good sees so much more in everyday life, and lives a much richer existence than the one who remains passive in the doldrums of routine." Those words, contained in the letter written by Liz's birth mother to The New York Foundling, were actually written by my own first mother about me. That letter is ninety-nine percent *my* birth mother's words, verbatim.

How lucky I was, like Liz, to be so loved. My birth mother, who was a schoolteacher and a deeply religious woman, did not believe she could offer me the life she thought I deserved, and so she finally did sign those papers, relinquishing her parental rights. She told the social workers at The New York Foundling that she had broken up with my birth father months before she realized she was pregnant, and so decided not to involve him. To this day, he probably does not know I exist.

A month later, I was adopted by Joe and Trudy Kearney and immediately had not only two new parents but also a brother and a sister, who were adopted as well. The three of us kids came from different families, but all of us were placed with our mom and dad through The New York Foundling in New York City. We lived in a little town called LaGrange, about seventy-five miles north of Manhattan. The fictional town of New Hook is in the same region—just west of Red Hook in New York State's Hudson Valley. I was brought, as Liz was, into my birth mother's dream family: affectionate, close-knit, Roman Catholic, living in the country. I was surrounded by books and music. My mom was a nurse and, in her younger years, a painter. My father was a teacher and then an elementary school principal. I had an older brother and sister who watched over me, and who today rank among my closest friends.

So the first two books of the trilogy mirror my own life in many ways, although growing up I didn't know anyone else (beside my siblings) who was adopted—I didn't have a Cathy or a Jan or a Jade, friends who understood my longing to know where I came from because they had similar questions themselves. (Luckily I did have a best friend, who is still very much a part my life, who saw me through all the trials and joys of growing up.) But the subject of adoption was avoided in my home much the way it is in Liz's. My siblings and I were Joe and Trudy's *children;* the word "adopted" was left out of conversations with anyone from outside our immediate family. I understand now that this was done out of love alongside a fierce sense of loyalty felt by all of us. I was the one who continuously wondered about my origins, especially about the woman who gave me life, though I learned pretty early on to keep my curiosity to myself.

Inside the four walls of our house, we would talk about the facts of our adoptions—what Mom and Dad were doing when they got the phone calls from The Foundling announcing the child they'd been hoping for was there, ready to be picked up; what few facts they'd been told about our ethnicities. But once the subject of feelings came up—confusion, pain, longing, or plain old curiosity—the conversation petered out or someone changed the subject. To ask about birth parents was disloyal, as it might have meant that Mom and Dad weren't "good enough." It took me, and thus Liz McLane, years to realize that wanting to know who your birth mother is has nothing to do with how much you love your parents. My family, like Liz's, finally came to understand that, too.

At first I resisted writing *When You Never Said Goodbye*. One hesitation came from the idea of reliving the emotional rollercoaster of searching for one's blood relatives. Did I, through Liz, really want to go for that ride again? One major obstacle I ran into during those years of my own search was my birth surname: Smith. (How I discovered my surname is too long a story to tell here.) Searching for a woman with the most popular surname in the United States is a bit daunting, to say the least. Liz, of course, discovers this as well. (While I'm on the subject of names: readers might remember that Liz's given name is Elizabeth Ann. Elizabeth Ann was the name of my birth mother, who as an adult went by Liz.)

At the same time, I knew that if I were to write it, this book would be the only one of the three that did not largely parallel my own story. I could not end Liz's search the way my own ended. After the eight-year quest for my birth mother, I discovered at age thirty-five that she had died of breast cancer years before, when I was nineteen. She was dead. It leveled me. I would never know Elizabeth Ann Smith. As the writer, I had the power to keep Liz from that fate. I could allow her birth mother to explain and express herself, to say "I love you"—even if Liz didn't get to meet her. So when I decided to forge ahead with book three and Liz's own search, I didn't know exactly how it would end.

The results of my own search weren't completely bad news: I did find blood relatives, including an aunt and uncle, a half-brother and half-sister, and many cousins. They all knew about me and welcomed me with an enthusiastic love that lasts to this day. And I look so much like my birth mother that when we met for the first time it seemed (they told me) as if I were a ghost, Elizabeth alive again in their midst. It was all a miracle. That said, I am still coming to terms with the idea that I will never meet my first mother. Maybe I'll never completely be at peace with that fact.

After struggling with the ending of the book, I realized that in order for it to ring emotionally true, I needed to find a way for Liz's birth mother to be alive and able to express her love for her daughter, and yet not be "available." This would enable me to tap into my own emotions that came with discovering how much my own birth mother had loved me *and* that she was dead. The idea of making Liz's mother a nun was something that had been in the back of my mind all along, but I kept resisting it. Who would believe it, a woman becoming a nun in the twenty-first century? Then I did some research and discovered that there are a few small convents in the United States that are thriving—and growing. Maybe it wasn't totally out of the question, the idea of Liz's first mother becoming a religious sister.

On a whim I decided to read a book that had been on my shelf for years, *The Name of the Rose* by Umberto Eco, about fourteenth-century monks. Because some monks, like some nuns, are cloistered, the book seemed like a promising choice. Perhaps it would guide me. It turned out that the paperback had a bookmark inside it from New York University, where my dad earned his undergraduate degree. The book must have been his. That was my sign! The rest of Liz's story flowed after that.

Here's what I know about Liz McLane's future. She will become a published poet. (After all, poetry is a gift both of our birth mothers wished for us.) She'll stay in New York City. She will always be rich in family and friends. That family will expand in time when she meets her birth mother's sisters and brother, and her cousins related to her by blood. Occasionally, she will spot new photos of her birth mother on the convent's website, and swear that Sister Dorothy is waving hello. She and Tim? I think they'll stay together. And always, she will be Lizzie, beloved daughter of Margaret and Patrick McLane, devoted sister to Kate and Bob. My blessed and plucky girl.

Notes

"A Guide to This Book's Poetics," "Suggested Books on Poetry and on Adoption," as well as a Teacher's Guide, all by Meg Kearney, can be downloaded at no cost from the publisher's website: www.perseabooks.com, and from www.megkearney.com.

Most of the names of bands, songs, and song lyrics mentioned in this book are written by Meg Kearney, including "When You Never Said Goodbye." (See pages 269–270, for the full lyrics to this song. Download the song at www.megkearney.com.) References are made to two songs by other artists: "You've Got a Friend" by Carole King (in "Ms. R in the Park," p. 49) and "My Father's Eyes" by Livingston Taylor (Journal Entry #2212, p. 189).

The names of professors and classes offered at NYU are also fictional, as is the bar called "The Rock."

About adoption registries: there are several websites that offer adoption search services. These sites maintain databases of adoptees, birth parents, and birth siblings who register their names and personal details with hope of finding a match. Some are national, some are statewide. The oldest reunion registries (both existed before the Internet) are the International Soundex Reunion Registry (ISRR), which is free; and the Adoptees' Liberty Movement Association (ALMA), which requires a fee before any information is released. For people adopted in New York State, there is also the Adoption and Medical Information Registry, run by the New York State Department of Health. Most sites are free, but watch for fees (some are hidden) if you decide to register. In order for there to be a match, both you and the person you're looking for must be registered on the same site. And sometimes the "match" turns out to be a mistake. Many sites will also connect you with a paid searcher, which can cost several thousand dollars. I suggest anyone deciding to go that route use only a searcher who can be recommended by someone trusted, and who asks for compensation only after successfully finding blood relatives.

In "Journal Entry #2167: January 10" (p. 30), the book Liz gives to Jan is *Drive, They Said: Poems About Americans and Their Cars,* edited by Kurt Brown (Milkweed, 1994).

"Torn" (p. 120) mentions a poem called "The Otter"; it's by Seamus Heaney, found in his collection, *Field Work* (Farrar, Straus & Giroux, 1976).

Pablo Neruda's poem "Horses" is mentioned in "April First" (p. 199). The poem can be found in *Full Woman, Fleshly Apple, Hot Moon: Selected Poems of Pablo Neruda* (HarperCollins, 1997: Stephen Mitchell, translator).

The Sisters of the Joyful Resurrection is an imaginary order of nuns inspired by several exisiting convents. In doing my research, I was surprised to find that young women in the twenty-first century are still entering the religious life (though not in the numbers they did in the past). The Dominican Sisters of St. Cecilia in Nashville, Tennessee, might be the fastest-growing order. At the time of this writing (2016), the average age of women entering the Sisters of St. Cecilia is twenty-three; the average age of the Sisters is thirty-six. Growing steadily in numbers, they are mostly college-educated women and many are teachers.

In Journal Entry #2222 (p. 235), Kate reads aloud about semi-cloistered communities. She is quoting from the website of the Daughters of the Immaculate Heart of Mary, an actual convent in Syracuse, New York. This site has excellent information about religious callings, life, vows, and leaving one's family behind to enter a convent: http://www.ihm daughters.org/site/822867/page/4134480.

Lyrics to the Song "When You Never Said Goodbye"

BY MEG KEARNEY

When You Never Said Goodbye

Had that dream again of asters
and black birds—you like a page torn—
just outside my door.
The wind stirs
and the leaves all let go.
Rushed out to greet you,
your face turned to snow.

CHORUS:

Wish I could climb inside
myself, tumble down
  tumble down
to a past I never knew—
maybe I'd reach the day
when maybe you said *Be good,*
when maybe you said *Don't cry,*
when maybe you said
  I love you—
when you never said goodbye.

Thought I saw you through a window
one April—there by the gold trees—
turned out you were me.
The wind blows
as though a mother-ghost.
I was still sea-borne
and you were my coast.

(CHORUS)

Once I met the great wizard
of heart-ache—his mask was the sea—
I pled for his pity.
The wind blurs
then snuffs the star lights out.
There are just some things
it can't live without.

(CHORUS)

Scan here to listen to a performance of the song and
for more information about the Lizzie McLane novels.

Acknowledgments

This is not a book I intended to write, back when I wrote *The Secret of Me* and *The Girl in the Mirror*. It was my editor and publisher at Persea Books, Karen Braziller, who believed Lizzie McLane must pursue her search for her birth mother: thus the trilogy was born. As difficult as it was for me to enter that territory with Lizzie, some heaven-sent signs and Karen's persistence urged me and Lizzie forward. I'm grateful for that now. (Lizzie is, too.) So thanks to Karen for being so tenacious and enouraging; and to publisher Michael Braziller, Jonah Fried in marketing, and to Rita Lascaro, designer and compositor. Thanks as well to my agent, Elaine Markson.

Thanks also to Jessica Flynn, former Undergraduate Programs Manager at NYU, for introducing me to Alexis Alvarado, Michael Frazier, and Fiona Wang, all freshmen living in Goddard Hall in the fall of 2013. A special thanks goes to Alexis, Michael, and Fiona for the tour of their dorm and a great conversation at Klong over lunch; plus for their answers to my questions via email (and for Michael's photos and patience when the questions kept coming).

My Spanish is very elementary, and so I could not have done without the enthusiastic help of poet María Luisa Arroyo, who helped me with some of the words and phrases in this book. My aunt, Nellie Kearney, also came to my aid in this regard.

Many people have supported me during the writing of *When You Never Said Goodbye* and in all of my literary endeavors: my beloved husband Gabriel Parker (my number-one supporter and cheerleader); Lita Judge (who was also this book's first reader and gave me invaluable feedback); Dave Judge; Beth Grosart Little (another first reader and great Lizzie fan); Maureen Petro (who assured me at a crucial moment that readers would understand and accept Sister Dorothy's calling to be a nun); Meg Dunn de Pulido; Laure-Anne Bosselaar; Deborah Smith Bernstein; Jett (proofreader extraordinaire) and Shelley Whitehead; Donald Hall; Fran Graffeo & Carol Hohman; Kathi Aguero (with a nod to her book *Daughter Of*); Kyle Potvin; Laura Williams McCaffrey; Laban Carrick Hill; Mark

Turcotte; Steve Huff; Anne-Marie Oomen; Ann Angel; Sarah Dunlap; Howard Levy; Martha Rhodes; Dave Capella; and—always—Jacqueline Woodson. Thanks, too, to Tanya Whiton and the entire community at the Solstice MFA in Creative Writing Program of Pine Manor College.

Writing this book also inspired me to create lyrics for the song "When You Never Said Goodbye." Thanks to Cornelius Eady for giving me advice about my first draft, and a *deep bow* to my song collaborators Beth Grosart Little and Chris Little for setting those lyrics to music. Beth also lent the song her stunning voice, and Chris his guitar playing. Colin McCaffrey offered up his own recording studio for the final cut, and was both our sound engineer and fiddler. I couldn't be more blown away by what these friends have done with my words, or more grateful. Check out the song through the link on my website, www.megkearney.com.

A huge hunk of appreciation also goes to Koke Fedorowicz, Nancy Ferrara, and the Ferrara family for "adopting me" and letting me use their cabin in the White Mountains of New Hampshire every August; and especially to Natalia Ferrara, a young and talented filmmaker, who created the book's trailer. I'm also grateful to actors Ali Lee and Daphne Greaves for lending their talents to make that fabulous trailer. Thanks also to Ruth and Jack Cook, formerly of Franconia, New Hampshire, for coming to my rescue in that cabin with homemade food, fascinating conversations about adoption, and a laptop loan during a crucial stretch in the writing of this book. Thanks also goes to all of my friends at the Frost Place in Franconia, New Hampshire, where I "grew up" as a poet.

As always, Wendy Freund [MSEd, LCSW], my social worker in the Adoption Unit at The New York Foundling, must be acknowledged for her enthusiam and support. She's been Lizzie's champion from the start. Wendy has now retired from The Foundling, but continues on with her private practice, with a special focus on artists and members of the adoption triad.

I dreamed of being a writer beginning in second grade, but never would have succeeded if not not for my parents' encouragement and my entire family's continued countenance. They have my gratitude and love always.

About the Author

MEG KEARNEY was born in the borough of Manhattan in New York City, and immediately placed into foster care under the auspices of The New York Foundling. At the age of five months, she was adopted and brought to live with her new parents and two older (also adopted) siblings in LaGrange, a town located in New York's Hudson Valley.

Kearney writes poetry for both adults and young adults, including *The Secret of Me* and *The Girl in the Mirror,* the first two novels in the Lizzie McLane trilogy. In 2010, *Home By Now,* her second collection of poems for adults, won the PEN New England L.L. Winship Award and was a finalist for the Paterson Poetry Prize and *Foreword Magazine's* Book of the Year. Among her other books are *An Unkindness of Ravens* (poetry for adults) and *Trouper* (a critically acclaimed picture book for children, illustrated by E. B. Lewis). Kearney's poems—and occasionally a story and an essay—have appeared in myriad literary journals and anthologies, and have been nominated for a Pushcart Prize four times. Garrison Keillor has read her poems on his national radio show, "The Writer's Almanac," and included her work in his anthology, *Good Poems: American Places.* Former U.S. poet laureate Ted Kooser also selected one of her poems for his "American Life in Poetry" column.

Before becoming founding director of the Solstice Low-Residency Master of Fine Arts in Creative Writing Program at Pine Manor College in Chestnut Hill, Massachusetts, Kearney was Associate Director of the National Book Foundation, sponsor of the National Book Awards, in New York City. She also taught poetry at The New School University (New York). A long time ago, she conducted power-plant tours for students and adults as part of her job at an electric utility in New York's Hudson Valley.

Kearney frequently visits schools and college classrooms nationwide, where she reads her poetry and discusses craft. She often is a speaker at literary and adoption conferences as well. She lives in New Hampshire with her husband; their three-legged dog, Trouper; their three-legged cat, Hopkins; and—oddly—their four-legged cat named Magpie. Visit her website: www.megkearney.com.